AF361235

My Ottawa Eagle

My ottawa Eagle

In search of the Soulmate

Virginie T.

Translated by Mustapha Naceur

© 2020. T. Virginie

My Eagle Ottawa

Chapter 1

Apenimon

I return from work in no hurry, driving on the winding path through the mountain on autopilot. It's the same thing every day. My job with the island's police is rewarding, but somewhat monotonous. In Manitoulin, there is no crime or traffic. Only petty theft among tourists or accidents that require an investigation to find out the circumstances, which are usually closed quickly.

Manitoulin is a small island with a limited number of inhabitants year-round, so everyone knows everyone. This phenomenon is reinforced by the fact that 90% of the natives belong to one of the six clans of the Ottawa tribe led by Tyee Pontiac, reinforcing my impression of being frozen in time.

My clan has always lived away from the others, at the top of the mountains, where the air is pure and where you are not likely to be disturbed by your neighbors. Our totem animal needs space and height, with an unobstructed view and thousands of fir trees. So, the mountains are the place to be. This had never bothered me before and allowed me to have an intimacy almost impossible to obtain in the valley. I am the descendant of a long line of warriors, hence my profession as a man of order, and our people have been at peace for a long time, which gave my solitude an escape from boredom. But lately, even the majestic landscape of trees bending in the gusts of wind is no longer enough to soothe my spirit. I feel like those trees that eventually crack and break down through hardship, without the protection of those around them. My heart is empty, on the verge of breaking, and my friends can do nothing for me. On the contrary, their presence only amplifies my malaise. They don't understand me. At just thirty years old, most of them only think about having fun and enjoying life, But I don't. I'm not a person who can do anything for myself. I'm looking for something deeper and infinitely more lasting.

Since our shaman, Achak, has found his soul mate, the sweet Isabelle, I pray to the Great Spirit to grant me this blessing as well. I have been waiting for this happiness for so long, since I was old enough to understand the importance of a soul mate. I heatedly wish it as I have been preparing myself for it for months, having already made room at home for the one created for me. I have also understood that destiny is playful. My wife is probably not part of the tribe, is not even Amerindian, just like Isabelle. As a security manager, I have attended every Pow Wow since I was old enough to drink, I have met all the members of the Pontiac tribe and all those from clans a little further away and more tourists than I can count. Yet my bride never showed up, she never showed up on the island. I would have met her a long time ago otherwise. So, I must change my tactics and stop standing still. It is also time for us to change our vision of life to embrace our destiny if we want to continue to prosper. Because, let's be honest. If we've always welcomed tourists with open arms, it's only out of self-interest. After all, they are the lifeblood of most Manitoulin Islanders, and while we are grateful, we remain wary of outsiders who wish to settle here, which is why there is so little diversity in the origins of our people. Like Achak, who refused to hire a foreign nanny for the chief's daughter. I remember his thoughts. He was convinced that her coming would bring misfortune to the tribe. A nanny who, ironically, eventually turned out to be his half. As for misfortune, Isabelle's arrival represented the biggest upheaval in his life and his happiness every day since they bonded. I must therefore be open-minded in my turn. I think it's high time for me to get out of my comfort zone and explore the surroundings around the island to try my luck. I'm heading to my boss, Tyee, to inform him of this, and I'm heading to his beautiful house next to Blue Jay Creek Park, which he manages as a tourist attraction.

I run into Isabelle and Aiyanna playing together in the garden. Our chief's daughter looks more and more like her mother, Aquene. Beautiful mischievous blue eyes and jet-black hair shining in the sun. She will make a magnificent lynx, all in finesse, which will make the most seasoned Ottawas crack in a few years from now with a simple glance. At the age of four, she cannot yet take on her animal form, we only get there around our tenth anniversary, and that's preferable, because this little tornado is already difficult to hold when she's on two legs, I can't imagine the mischief she'll show on all fours. Tyee's got a lot to worry about. I'm also noticing something that gives me a twinge, as it always does. Isabelle's belly is getting rounder every day. The announcement of her pregnancy on the day of the Pow Wow took us all by surprise, including Achak, who didn't know anything about it and had a hard time containing his joy. The French origins of our shaman's wife are betrayed by her skin as pale as ivory, but her place among us is no longer to be proven. She accepted our rites and customs without the slightest hesitation and I hope my companion will be as tolerant. Isabelle is part of the Ottawa tribe just like me and the tribe will welcome a baby lynx in the coming months. It will be a great moment for all of us and a great celebration will take place to celebrate this event. I ardently wish to experience the joy of fatherhood in my turn and I hope to go to this ceremony with my soul mate on my arm. This would be a major step forward in my dream of starting a family.

When you think of the lynx. There's Achak coming out of the huge family home, followed closely by his brother Tyee, our leader.

— Hello, Apenimon. You're looking well. It's good to see you, you hadn't left your mountains to visit us for too long. We only see you from afar during your patrols. What can we do for you?

— Hey, guys. How did you know I wanted something? Can't I come to you for the pleasure of your company?

Achak laughs as he takes his companion in his arms, placing his hands on her navel in a possessive gesture. Isabelle snuggles up against him, laying her hands on his. There is an obvious osmosis between them. I want to know the same alchemy with the one destined for me.

— The door will always be open to you and you know it. But you forget that the spirits speak to me, my friend. And you will not make me believe that you came down into the valley just to see our faces.

Tyee watches me observe the couple with a desire that I can't hide because it's so intense. I too want to hug the woman of my life and look at her rounded belly, irrefutable proof of our love.

— I figured you'd be coming to see me soon. I'm even surprised it didn't happen sooner. Well, I know you. We grew up together, don't forget that. You've wanted a companion for a long time, and Achak's union with his soul mate only rekindled your desire to find your true love, didn't it?

Yes, he does know me well. We made a lot of

mistakes together as kids. And even more so as a teenager. Have you ever seen a bobcat fly? You couldn't? No, not when it's carried through the air by my pet. But don't be nostalgic.

— That's right. I also believe that my soul mate is not on the island. If you'll both allow me, I'd like to go away for a while and try to find her. We're in a slow tourist season, so my colleagues will do fine without me.

The two brothers look at each other and communicate silently, only by looking at each other. They often do that. It's confusing and frustrating. How can you counter their arguments if you don't hear them? It is Achak who takes the floor again.

— You're probably right. Your soul mate is not among us, you would have discovered it by now with all the people you come across all day long. Besides, the fox clan hasn't taken any reprisals since Takhi's death. Her family has accepted the fact that she acted badly and knew her well enough to know that she died because she refused to submit. So you can go exploring quietly. We can get along just fine without you for a while. You're not as indispensable as you think you are!

Despite what she says, her sparkling eyes prove to me that I matter to them as much as they matter to me. His joke helps me relax. I didn't realize until that moment that the idea of this confrontation had gotten on my nerves. It would have been very bad for me if they had refused.

— Where do you plan to go?

— The Great Spirit remains vague in spite of my prayers. All I know is that I have to go to the northwest, which remains vague.

Achak nods his head. He knows something I don't know, no doubt about it. Logically, he communicates with all spirits without exception. Our shaman is very powerful and close to the totem spirits.

— Head for Kipawa Lake, but be very careful. You will find the object of your quest, but you will have to prove your worth to get it.

Ah, that's right. Spirits love riddles and mysteries. They keep us on our toes, but they never give us all the answers. It's up to us to decide which path we'll take to reach our goal, because after all, the path is as important as the destination. I didn't expect it to be. I have their blessings, which is very important to me, and most importantly, a clue as to where I will find the love of my life. For the first time, I'm touching my dream with my fingertips and I don't plan to miss it. It's up to me to do everything I can to make it happen now and I won't back down from any obstacle.

— I'm sorry I can't give you more details. I know it's not a lot of information.

— Don't worry about it. I wouldn't expect so much, so thank you. I could really use your help. Thanks to you, I'm not going in blind. My pet should be able to do the rest. He's as impatient as I am and will do everything in his power to find the one that belongs to us. I'll see you soon. I'll come and introduce you to my wife as soon as I get back.

— See you soon, Apenimon. And don't hesitate to call us if you need any help. We're here for you, even from afar. Bring your soul mate home.

I'm going back to my house to pack while I think about the shaman's warning. I should prove my worth. What did the spirits mean? I am a warrior, my strength and loyalty are no secret to anyone. Not from any ottawa, anyway. My soul mate is certainly outside this world, and as a matter of fact, my name will tell him nothing about me, I'll be just another man in those eyes. And value certainly doesn't depend only on physical strength, it takes more than that to impress a woman. I set off as soon as my travel bag is ready and loaded into the car, my head full of hope and questions. I can't wait to meet the woman who will fill my soul and that of my pet. I am ready to do anything to seduce her and keep her close to me.

Chapter 2

Cayla

Leaving on a whim in the middle of the Kipawa Lake Ancient Forest seemed like a good idea at the time. When the MFFP, the Ministry of Wildlife, Forests and Parks, proposed this mission, I thought "great, I will be able to combine my passion with my need for solitude". Now that I find myself in the middle of this vegetation that has been preserved for more than 400 years, certainly magnificent and lush, but completely lost, I am less convinced by my flash of genius. Solitude is nice, but certainly not when there are only trees as far as the eye can see and orientation is far from my strong point. I am still convinced that I had all the right reasons in the world to exile myself in this way, but it is no help to me when my map does not give me any information about my position. How do you read this thing? I have no idea where I am and my head is buzzing with parasitic thoughts, short-circuiting my rational, calm side. My last love affair ended with loss and smash and left me more bruised than I had told my family, leaving me full of bitterness. My parents thought that a change of scenery would help me bounce back and so supported me in my wish to go to the other side of the world, alone. Anyway, my family never liked Richard and it was essential for my mental health that I change my mind.

I am originally from Lorraine, where I discovered my passion: animals. Since I was very young, as far back as I can remember, I was in admiration of them and I forced my parents to go to the Amnéville zoo at least once a month. My parents knew the alleys by heart by dint of driving me there constantly and despite their weariness, they always acceded to my request. The zebras and tigers with their irregular black stripes, the white lions with their thick fur and all the other inhabitants of the animal park had captivated me at first glance, like all children I suppose, but more than anything else, I fell in love with the birds of prey. Their aviary is one of the largest in the world and their spectacle is simply breathtaking. Harris' huge falcons, fishing eagles and buzzards, among others, fly freely in an exceptional ballet that ends with a final flight of more than sixty birds simultaneously that leaves you speechless. For the little girl I was on my first visit, it was a revelation. I envied their freedom in the sky and their so majestic appearance. I felt as if I was tiny under these masters of the skies. So, I decided to become a veterinarian and work in this zoo. I studied, persevered and studied some more. I immersed myself in this universe with every fiber of my body, regularly putting my life as a carefree party student on hold and telling myself that I would make up for it later. While my crazy roommates dressed up to laugh, flirt and be honest, have sex, I immersed myself in my books on dog anatomy and animal behavior. I achieved my goal at age twenty-five and have never regretted my sacrifices.

Only here I am four years later away from home because I made the wrong choice. A bad choice from the beginning of my life and I find myself thousands of miles away from my family. If I do have one regret, it is that I gave in and put my heart before my brain. I should have gone on as before and listened to my head screaming at me not to do that. Dating my boss was a big mistake. And yet, it had started so well. The zoo director, Richard Watson, 10 years my senior, gradually gave me attention and I felt flattered. True, who wouldn't have been. Richard is rich, charismatic, pleasant to look at and I respect his work and his fight to save the species. We sailed in the same professional environment, which was an advantage for me. I naively thought I had found my alter ego. It was flattering to attract such a leading authority in his field. It started with small attentions: he kissed me instead of shaking my hand, he regularly came to the care centre to check that I didn't lack equipment, regularly asked my opinion on the animals to come... Then one day, everything became more concrete.

"I really like you, Cayla. I've been watching you for months now, and I've been telling myself that I'm your boss and that employee relations are not recommended, but I can't stay away from you anymore. "Come and have a drink with me.

I had thought about it, weighed the pros and cons, and finally agreed. His manly smile on firm, full lips and his eyes shining with desire for me had gotten the better of me. Our relationship had begun a year earlier with a fiery kiss. The kind of kiss that leaves you with wobbly legs and wet panties and I naively thought we would end our life together. Even though we didn't live together, we sometimes talked about babies. Finally, looking back, I realize that it was mostly me who envisioned this logical continuation of our love, while my lover systematically dodged the subject.

"I feel so good for you. Do you ever think of a little person who looks just like us? A mixture of you and me?

There's plenty of time to think about it, Cayla, there's no rush".

I didn't necessarily agree with that remark. After all, we were a decade apart and I sometimes wondered if his reluctance was not due to that fact. Richard is in his late 40s, and I suppose that made him hesitate when I thought, "This is the time to have a child," I thought. I didn't want Richard to be an "old" dad by taking our child to school. It's embarrassing when you say to a child, "Here's your grandpa," and he says, "That's my father. The reality had turned out to be much more painful and humiliating. He was not considering offspring at all, now or ever, and age was indeed an issue in our marriage, but it was not his, it was mine. Twenty-nine years is his age limit for his conquests.

I remember perfectly well that day that shook my life and changed my future. I went to surprise him. I was off that day and I had planned to meet him for lunch. I'm very happy about that. I was the one who was stunned, and not in the best sense of the word. I went home without knocking, as usual, and was paralyzed by the vision in front of me. Richard was sitting in the chair behind his desk, his fly open, a trainee moaning in his lap. It was my boss's voice that had brought me out of my torpor.

"Cayla, what are you doing here?

— That's all you have to say? Maybe you could pull your pants up.

— It's not what you think it is.

— It's not what you think? Well, let me guess. Our new reptile trainee wanted to feed your snake? "Forget it, kid, it's not an anaconda, it's a tiny little asp".

I left, slamming the door with the giggle of the

too-young lady and the crimson face of my now ex-child. This pitiful revenge did not relieve me, however, and coming to work the next day as if nothing had happened, after ignoring countless calls from the other idiot, it was revealed as torture, as all my colleagues knew the reason for our break-up. Their support and compassion in the face of Richard's betrayal only intensified my sense of suffocation in this place I had loved so much. I could no longer bear to walk down the aisles filled with happy families and colleagues who knew too much about my problems and Richard's sex life.

So that night, I set out to find a new job that would allow me to get away from it all while keeping in touch with the birds of prey. I wasn't ready to forget my priorities. After a lot of research, I came across the website of the Ministère de la Forêt, de la Faune et des Parcs du Québec. The MFFP was looking for veterinarians specializing in poultry to study eagles and thus better adapt their protection on the territory. Neither one nor two, I applied and was hired. Richard did try to hold me back, claiming that I had advance notice, but the threat of filing a harassment complaint, via text message, got the better of him. This is how I find myself in the riding of Temiscaming, with my camping equipment and observation gear in a small hand trailer, driving along Lake Kipawa through hemlock groves with yellow birch, a distant cousin of our common fir trees, to observe the majestic eagles that nest there. I feel laughed at in the middle of this immense landscape, some specimens reaching more than 30 meters, but also in peace. The weeks after the breakup had been morally trying and Richard's insistence on holding me back, God knows why, hadn't helped. My resignation put a definitive end to this page of my life and this peaceful silence is a real soothing balm for my bruised heart.

Chapter 3

Apenimon

Fatigue is felt after driving for four hours, three-quarters of the journey, forcing me to stop in North Bay. The place is rather deserted at the end of the day. I find myself in a small, simple but functional hotel with a comfortable room and an adjoining bathroom. It's strange to be far from the island. I had never left it, except during my years at the police academy, and this change of scenery, even if it's for a good cause, stresses me out. All I need is a hearty meal and a few hours of sleep to get back on track towards my destiny. I'm feverishly impatient, but I won't reach my goal if I fall asleep at the wheel and my empty stomach won't stop gurgling. So I go to the little grill restaurant next door to get my fill before taking a well-deserved nap. The big pickups parked in the adjacent parking lot make me nervous. It's not the vehicles themselves, but rather the load they are carrying. There are cages on the rear trunk, awkwardly covered with a tarp, as well as locked metal crates, probably filled with shotguns. As a hunter myself, and one of the best, in all humility, I don't like this imbalance of power. What can an animal do when faced with a weapon that can hit it from several meters away? My beast shivers in my head at this unpleasant thought. I doubt that men who possess such an arsenal, fight fair, and when you hunt for food, you certainly don't need a cage to lock up your dead prey. Poaching may be prohibited, but wildlife trafficking is very lucrative and encourages unscrupulous people to defy the law. I do not intend to linger here or get involved in matters that do not concern me, but I will contact the county authorities to inform them of my suspicions once I get home.

At this late hour, there are few people in the establishment and I can easily find a table to sit at. As on Manitoulin Island, this part of Quebec is mainly inhabited by Amerindians, which allows me to go relatively unnoticed. Even with a matte complexion and the same accent, I could easily pass for a local guy. At least, that's what I thought until the waitress came up to me and imposed a formal interrogation on me about anything other than my choice of menu. Besides, she was reluctant to give me the menu before she had answers about a situation that had nothing to do with her.

— Hello. I haven't seen you around here before. Where are you from?

Why that suspicious, highly disturbing look? She's

looking at me like a juicy piece of meat that's in front of her while she's on a diet. Don't they ever get tourists in this town? On closer inspection, it's a small snack bar that doesn't look like much with only a few men looking at me like a curious beast and this middle-aged waitress who doesn't seem very friendly. Visitors shouldn't crowd at the gate. Her blonde mop tangled in a shapeless bun and her screaming lipstick barely distract my eyes from her clean, but not at all fresh, outfit. Might as well play the game and get it over with. I have nothing to hide or blame myself for and this should be over soon.

— I just came in from Lake Huron.

— And what are you doing in our neck of the woods?

— Sightseeing. I'm just passing through.

— Where do you go if you're just passing through?

That's enough now. I'm willing to be cooperative, but there are limits. I'm a warrior, not a defendant in a police station. I usually ask the questions, and this woman lacks the subtlety of poking hard at the men at the counter. I came here to eat, not to give a lecture on why I'm here at this particular time. I take a brief look at the menu and order the specialties, cutting short her intrusion into my private life.

— Could I have a smoked meat sandwich and poutine, please?

She looks at me sideways, unhappy with my dodge, but finally gives up after taking another look at the hunters. Obviously, they know each other. She answers in a dry tone.

— I'll get it to you right away. With water?

— That would be perfect.

She turns not without a suspicious glance in my direction. Her comments, supported by the reason I'm here, have drawn more than adequate attention from the hunters. They seem nervous and squinting, and the waitress is probably trying to identify a threat to them. The animal welfare kind of thing. I stop staring at them when my plate arrives. I don't want to get into trouble, that's not why I'm here, but I make a mental note to warn the authorities without fail.

I take advantage of my meal to think of my companion. I wonder what she looks like. I have no preference for her looks. I don't have one type of girl that attracts me more than another, as long as she's natural and I'm confident. I'm sure the spirits have reserved the perfect woman for me. I'm more demanding about character, though. Isabelle is an adorable woman and I appreciate her a lot, but she is too shy and reserved for my taste. I would like a strong woman with a strong character who can stand up to me and who doesn't hesitate to make her own choices without fear of consequences. My animal is a predator and is far from being tamed. He and I need a companion who tells us what she thinks, who takes the initiative, and who is not afraid to put us in our place when we need her. I swallowed my meal in one go without even noticing it, so much my thoughts were monopolized by my soul mate, as often. I pay and go home right away to go to bed. I'm getting tired and a restful sleep will allow me to leave tomorrow morning, without wasting any more time.

There is a lot of fog around me. It's hard to make out anything in this mash. I'll have to transform; my vision will be much better and the weather won't bother me above the clouds any more. Only I can't do it. I'm stuck in my man's body. Something's holding me down, motionless. I can't move an inch; I can't move an inch. Even my head is stuck in an unnatural position, looking upwards, so that I can't even see my body, only the treetops and a blue sky clear of clouds. Suddenly I hear a voice. A bewitching voice that speaks to me with such affection. I guess a figure nearby, but I can't make out its features. It has to be her. The right person for me is there. She tells me to stay calm, that she will take care of me. It's nice to hear her say that she's going to take care of me after all these years of taking care of others, but the truth is, it's my job to take care of my wife. Unfortunately, I sense a threat looming around us. Why am I paralyzed? A mere bystander? It's as if I'm outside my body, without seeing myself. And why is my bride a shadow? I must defend my wife, it's my duty. I'm an Ottawa warrior and a policeman, I'm fit to protect her, as long as my body responds to me. Danger is closing in, sneaky. And suddenly everything turns red in front of my eyes, darkening my vision and making it useless. Blood, blood spreads all around me and my love starts to move away, disappearing from my field of vision. No. There's no way I'm losing my half, not now, not when I've just found it. I'm struggling with my torpor. I'm fighting my own body to move; I have to save it.

I'm so fidgety I end up... falling out of bed. A dream, it was just a dream. No, not just a dream. A warning message from the spirits. I must hurry. My companion is in great danger. I must find her and quickly if I don't want this nightmare to become reality. The alarm clock on the bedside table reads six thirty and I can guess the first rays of the sun through the gaps in the shutters. It's impossible to transform myself discreetly from here to take flight. This is the most important rule of my tribe, no one must know of our powers outside the clans. A wild animal coming out of a hotel room would be a mess.

I'm not wasting a second. I throw my stuff in the trunk of my car, go through the hotel reception to return the keys and pick up, thanks to the concierge, a vital piece of information: the address of a quiet place. I get back behind the wheel and head for the Widdifield Forest indicated by the receptionist, only a few kilometers away.

I leave my vehicle on a small path along the large fir trees. Everything is quiet, no hikers or campers in sight, as the hotel employee assured me. It's just perfect. I undress out of sight, turn into a spray of sparks and gain height. My beast is delighted to spread its wings and feel the wind on its head and along its plumage. However, it is not enjoying this moment of freedom as usual. No circle on the spot to spot prey, no stake dive to the ground to get an adrenaline rush. We hunt for a bigger booty, the biggest of treasures. Our companion is waiting for us at Lake Kipawa. She needs us. Lake Kipawa is huge, over three hundred square kilometers, and stretches across five different townships. Finding my soul mate in the middle of such a vast territory will be like looking for a needle in a haystack. Fortunately, my bird of prey is used to spot a little mouse in the middle of a forest. His sight is the best in the animal kingdom. So my animal runs like an arrow towards the body of water a hundred kilometers southeast of my position, on the lookout for the slightest sign of my companion's presence.

Chapter 4

Cayla

What a horrible night! I've never been a big fan of camping, but this is the best. The ground on which I pitched my tent, which had seemed so flat the day before, turned out to be all bumps and bumps. What's more, my air mattress only has an inflatable in the name. It's mainly deflatable to be more precise, which allowed me to appreciate the beautiful granite stones just under my back, giving me a massage that is all the more unpleasant on my lumbar vertebrae. Not being a geologist, I couldn't be ecstatic about their beauty, which would probably have compensated for my resentment of their incredible hardness. Of course, there were also the little animals of all kinds that managed to get into my makeshift home despite the mosquito net, and I am not an entomologist either. It seems that I chose my vocation badly. I like to have company in my bed, but I prefer it firm, warm and muscular and not slimy, hairy or prickly like the caterpillars, spiders and other cheerful creatures that had invited themselves into my duvet. In this case, I might as well sleep alone. As for those who praise the silence of the night, where do they live to say that? Because I can certify that it wasn't the silence that oppressed me, but the noise. The sound of the wind through the high trees and something unimaginable without having experienced it yourself. My awakening is therefore difficult and far too early for my taste in view of my short hours of sleep. The sun is just beginning to appear through the hemlock, cedar and maple trees that surround me, giving the place a somewhat gloomy air, full of ghostly shadows and the sound of twigs cracking under the paws of invisible animals. I may come from the country, but I'm not a wilderness camper, and I'm frankly starting to regret setting out on this adventure. To tell the truth, this is a first for me and the experience is proving to be less pleasant than I imagined. I get up with difficulty from my makeshift mattress that looks like a pancake again and that I certainly won't regret when I get home, aching almost everywhere. I had no idea that the human body had so many muscles! I turn on the stove to make myself a coffee. After a black cup of my favourite drink, everything will be better. It'll give me the boost I need to face this second day in the forest. Come on, girl. Shake it off, you didn't come to Canada for the holidays, you came to study the big raptors in the region. The MFFP is counting on my report to put in place better species preservation strategies such as observatories or limiting tourism in certain areas. This is a noble and important cause that is well worth the trouble I am taking on. After donning a trellis and a fleece jacket over my favourite blue T-shirt, I conscientiously fold up my tent. I mean, I try. The pop-up system is a fantastic innovation for setting up your igloo in thirty seconds. The disadvantage is that it takes a good half hour to fold it up. You have to be an engineer to be able to superimpose the three rings or what? Why can I only make two loops? It's no longer a small compact circle that fits in the blanket, but a big oval with me. Like all self-respecting modern women, I take out my smartphone to watch an explanatory video, just to finally solve the puzzle and move on. Only, it's bad luck, I don't understand. Nothing, nothing, not even the slightest little bar to give me hope. When I thought about it, my colleagues had indeed warned me that in order to have a network, I had to stand by the lake. I'm too deep in the vegetation to have bars, so I have to manage to solve this puzzle worse than a 9×9 rubik's cube. I end up winning after a fierce battle between me and my tent and a good ten minutes of extra puzzles, so the sun is high in the sky when I'm finally ready to go again. Something to think about tonight. Do I really have to put this tent up? The memory of last night's strange noises tells me yes. I'm no coward, but I'm still alone in the middle of nowhere, and the forest is home to moose, black bears, muskrats and other animals. The kind of animals I'd rather not meet in the dark. Not in broad daylight either. So, the tent offers a semblance of protection that is not negligible, even if when faced with a determined wild animal, its protection will become relative.

As for me, I'm here to observe eagles and it's time for me to get to work. So, I continue to go deeper into the vegetation to reach a clear, high rocky platform that I spotted on the topographic maps I studied with the team before I left. This will be the ideal place to observe the surrounding treetops and get a great view of the entire area. The trip is long and tiring, and I can't feel my shoulder when I pull my damn trailer to reach my goal. But the view was worth it, it's breathtaking. From my high promontory, I can see much of the ancient forest of Lake Kipawa, but also the lake itself, all surmounted by a beautiful cloudless blue sky illuminated by a bright sun that reflects off the water like a myriad of stars. I can see sandhill cranes, woodcocks and brown-capped chickadees in my binoculars near the shore, but what fascinates me most is the pair of eagles I see on top of a hemlock. They are side by side, proudly erect above the rest of the world, their nest visible a few branches below. Eagles represent my ideal vision of the couple: once they have found each other, they remain faithful until the death of one of them, build their habitat together and look after their offspring in harmony, incubating the eggs and taking turns hunting. A fair division of labor too rare in humans. That's why I'm here. This spectacle must endure over time at all costs. A little further on, I see another bird of prey circling, perhaps in search of food. That's strange, isn't it? Eagles tend to be territorial. Apart from pairs, you never see two eagles on the same hunting ground. This lone pair should be no less than a mile away as the crow flies, and might feel threatened by the presence of a male. I am so caught up in my reflection that I am startled when a thud resounds in the calm of the forest. A detonation resounds in this peaceful place, making all the surrounding birds fly away. My heart pounds and is far from calming down when the bird of prey that I was watching just a moment earlier, starts to fall from the sky at a crazy pace, beating frantically with one wing, making it whirl, but barely slowing down its fall. Oh my God! I helplessly witness the worst nightmare that a protector and nature lover like me can see. Somebody deliberately shot the animal. I'm in the middle of a protected area and yet a poacher has just shot the poor animal. The bird bounces off the high branches of trees like a rag doll and disappears from my field of vision in the middle of the vegetation. Pushed in my direction by the wind and its disorderly movements, it must not have crashed more than a kilometer or two from my position. I absolutely have to do something. After all, I'm a vet, so if he's still alive I must try to save him by all means. Without even thinking about the potential risks of what I'm about to do, I literally turn my trailer upside down to empty it in one go and drive down the rocky cliff I'd climbed so laboriously earlier as fast as I could, almost breaking my neck several times in my rush as I slid over unstable rocks. Quickly, quickly! Once down, I try to find my way around, which proves to be complicated. Decidedly, me and orientation are two. Only, I don't have all day if I want to intervene in time. Seen from below, everything looks the same: trees as far as the eye can see. I stand with my back to the promontory and close my eyes to visualize the scene. On the left, he fell westwards. I resume my run, already out of breath, hoping not to be too late with the bird. I am soon disoriented and stop my sprint. I don't know where to go. I pray for a clue when the silence is broken by a faint chatter. Then nothing more. Perhaps I imagined him so much I hope to rescue him? It could also be the couple of eagles in the tree, but never mind. With luck, it's the wounded animal. I resume my run towards what I believe to be the origin of the cry in the hope of saving him.

Chapter 5

Apenimon

I was taken for a sucker! As if there was the slightest resemblance between us! Somebody's been doing target practice, with me as the target. I've been wounded before, and more than once. After all, I'm a warrior and a policeman. But fighting has always been done with bare hands or with squeeze shots in face-to-face encounters with equal weapons or in training sessions where the wounds were accidental. This is different. I took a bullet in the wing in mid-air, when I was at my most vulnerable. The aim of the attack was to harm me without my being able to defend myself, and it succeeded. The landing was hard and more than painful. Well, the term landing is probably a bit of an exaggeration. Instead, I crashed to the ground like a stone. Fortunately, the trees slowed my descent thanks to my magnificent (OK, it's all relative) bouncing off the branches, which are much less leafy than they look, like a marble in a pinball machine. The ottawa may heal incredibly fast, but you don't rise from the dead anyway. With a fall like that, I could have broken my neck on the ground and been done with it. The branches plucked feathers from me as I passed, causing other injuries, this time minor, but I am alive. I hurt all over, but I'm alive. In fact, the sharp pain in my humerus confirms it. As a fighter, I've always been taught that pain is a good sign. As long as you're in pain, there's hope. My bone is probably broken. Nothing serious, as far as I can tell. A fracture heals itself, and quickly, for my people. The problem is that the projectile I was hit with probably got stuck in the flesh, preventing healing from the Ottawa magic, and I can't turn back into a broken bone either. Anyway, I'm in trouble up to my neck, but on the bright side, alive. I mean, for now.

Only a miracle could save me permanently. I can't stay on the floor ad vitam aeternam where I'll end up starving or being attacked by a predator against which I would be vulnerable and I still can't extract the bullet with my beak. My faint screams will eventually attract hikers, hopefully. Unless it's those damn poachers coming in. When I said that some of them are unscrupulous... I was hovering over the Ancient Forest of Lake Kipawa. This is a protected area where hunting is, in fact, prohibited and punishable by law. This should never have happened. It remains to be seen whether it is poachers who hunt trophies, and if so, I will end up dead to be stuffed (they will get a big surprise. Once dead, you automatically revert to human form, which would blow your secret away), or if they're looking for new species for rich sponsors who are forming their own clandestine zoo, in which case it wasn't smart of them to stuff me to such a height. It reminds me of the North Bay hunters. They had cages in the back of their vehicles, big enough to hold a specimen like my animal, and it's not too far from here. Cages meant capture. If it is them, all hope is not lost. They won't leave without their prey, and most importantly, they will cure me so they can sell me. On the other hand, shooting me at such a height is a real nonsense. Novices perhaps? They didn't look like novices. I'll know how to get out of their enclosure once I'm back on my feet. I'll just have to wait until nightfall to transform and open my prison. It's no big deal. But someone has to take care of me first.

I got out of my thoughts by the creaking branches nearby. Hurried and disorderly footsteps, as if in panic. The poachers are afraid of being caught red-handed in a forbidden hunting area and hurry to finish their dirty work? Or tourists have seen me fall and want to rescue me? Either way, I need help, whoever it is. I pray to the spirits to come to my aid in some way and not to make wrong assumptions, because my life depends on it. I cry out a little louder with my last strength, to direct possible help to me. I was not expecting the vision that is offered to me as I emerge from the foliage. A woman. A beautiful woman with a necklace shining with every ray of sunshine that crosses the undergrowth. Her pendant catches my attention. It represents an eagle, its wings spread, two superb sparkling citrines as eyes. That's where the sparkle came from that attracted me like a magnet to this corner of the forest, making me miss the presence of malevolent characters in the half-light. Seen from the sky, it was only a shining point on the horizon and I wanted to find out where it came from, I felt the urge, seeing only that, but I fell before reaching it. Most of the ottawa of my tribe have a mammal as a totem animal and locate their mate through their sense of smell, but me, I belong to the only bird clan of the Pontiac tribe, I am a bird with exceptional eyesight, so it is normal that it is my eyes that identify my soul mate and it is the person right in front of me without the slightest doubt.

She is very beautiful, of a subtle but undeniable beauty. She looks rather tall to me, but on the other hand, I'm spread out on the floor like a vulgar chicken with its wings cut off, so it doesn't mean much. Her electric blue T-shirt sticks to her skin because of the perspiration due to her probable run, drawing her shapes like a second skin. She has a generous bosom in a lace bra whose floral patterns I can guess under the cotton fabric. A feast for the eyes. I thank my eagle for her exceptional sight allowing me to perceive the smallest details of her anatomy. And her face! It is quite simply a work of art. A fine face with chiseled cheekbones, framed by strands of chestnut hair in various shades ranging from light to caramel-colored strands that have escaped from his ponytail. She has a pulpy mouth of a pretty soft pink that I want to thumb over to test its softness, but what fascinates me most are her almond-shaped eyes. Thanks to my eagle, I can make out the flashes of green in the middle of her storm-grey eyes that captivate and hypnotize me. My bird of prey, just like me, is captivated by his vision and exults to have finally found his half. I have achieved my goal. On the other hand, I wanted to make a good first impression, so we'll come back. Instead of launching the seduction phase that I have been imagining for months "let me introduce myself to the most beautiful woman I have ever seen", I am nailed to the ground, clumsily leaning against a tree, stuck in my animal form.

I don't move while she watches me. I would like to say that I do not want to frighten her, but honestly, it is mostly because I am unable to do so. My benign plumage injuries have all but disappeared, although the feathers are still missing, but my wing throws at me horribly and the slightest movement is torture. The great warrior that I am is down. It is frustrating to be so helpless. Fortunately, as always among kindred spirits, she doesn't seem to be afraid of me. Curious, suspicious, but not afraid. And she's doing very well except for a jerky breathing due to her recent efforts to reach me as soon as possible. What an idiot! My dream wasn't about her, it was about me. It was my blood that I saw flowing and my wound that I felt during my nightmare, immobilizing me as I am at this moment. It is not I who must save my companion, but she who will help me. I understood everything upside down, just like Achak when the spirits sent him a vision of a great change. Clearly, when it comes to our companion, visions are never what they seem.

Chapter 6

Cayla

There's an eagle in front of me. But not just any eagle. A bald eagle, my favorite. I find him magnificent despite the unlikely situation I find myself in. He has a deep brown plumage that contrasts with his bright white head and tail and bright yellow legs and hooked beak, the same colour as his eyes that are scanning me. I have had close encounters with it in the zoo, but always in the presence of its keeper or trainer. The trainer is not tamed and is probably not used to human contact. So, I approach with caution to see the extent of the damage. If the animal gets scared, it can bite me badly with its powerful talons. I wouldn't want to find myself in the place of a prey in its claws. I'm not a fish, but if it feels threatened, my skin won't be able to withstand it. So, I make slow movements to spot the wounds the rifle and its fall must have made.

— Easy, boy. I mean you no harm. I'm here to help you. Please don't move and don't attack me. I'm just looking at you a little closer. I'm not your next meal, let alone your enemy.

The bird tilts its head to the side. That's strange. I almost feel like he understands me. I've never seen an eagle with such a gleam of intelligence in its eyes. They're clever and agile and quick learners, but this is different. I keep talking to him, hoping that my voice will calm him down and break the oppressive silence that surrounds us.

— My name is Cayla. I've only been working for the MFFP for a short time. It means Ministry of Wildlife, Forests and Parks. A great title to say I'm here for the animals in your situation. I came to study your species in this forest so that we can better protect you and your friends, and it looks like you need it.

As I continue my litany, I touch the wing that seems to be in good shape. Some primary remiges and small nursing blankets are missing, you can see where they were ripped off, but there are no wounds. That's odd. He must have already been missing some before his freefall descent. Looks like this bird's unlucky and not his first trouble. His chest is rising steadily, so he probably doesn't have any broken ribs, which is good news. I don't dare to touch its legs, a false move happens so quickly. Anyway, at first glance, tarsals, tibias and femurs seem intact, no distortion, everything is well aligned in a normal position. Finally, the only serious injury seems to result from the bullet he received, which caused a clearly visible hole on the top of his wing, where a trickle of blood flows continuously, staining and sticking his plumage. It doesn't really look like he's just fallen more than forty meters. If I were him, another one would certainly have died when the eagle in front of me is almost like a charm. It's a mystery to me. On the other hand, this is not really the time to think about that. I don't really feel like coming face to face with the one who shot that poor beast. I suppose the person responsible is a poacher and he might not be happy to see that there is a witness to his misdeed. Assuming it is a single person, which is not a certainty. Anyway, I might as well stay out of trouble and get out of here fast, but not without my patient.

— Take it easy, buddy. Stick, stick. There you go, that's perfect. Come on, please pretend as if it's prey.

I pick up a piece of wood about two feet long and six inches in diameter and throw it gently between his legs. As I planned, by reflex, the bird of prey grabs it with its claws. One less danger when I handle it. Suddenly I miss the zoo's care center. A thick leather glove would have been welcome. And if I'd thought about it before hurtling down the slope like crazy, I would have also taken the little blanket from my luggage to wrap it in and make it easier to handle. Truly, nature is not my element and is obscuring my common sense.

— That's good, don't move. I'm going to catch you now. Don't peck me, okay. I promise I'll be careful.

I gently press his wings against his body and, holding him at arm's length, put him on my little trailer. The eagle let himself be handled without the slightest resistance; I'm bluffed. He doesn't look like a wild animal; he doesn't have the instinctive reactions. He followed all my gestures with his eyes without losing a crumb, but he never showed any sign of distrust or aggressiveness! No shaking, no sign of a next peck and the stick is still stuck in his paws without the slightest clue that he is going to drop it to attack me.

I set off back to my camp without wasting time pulling my precious load to get away from the drop point so that I can heal him, my brain full of questions. The animal weighs no more than four or five kilos, but my arms still hurt and it takes me a long time to avoid all the holes and rocks so as not to shake it. At the bottom of the cliff, I realize that it will be impossible to mount the trailer without hurting its passenger. So, I leave it at the foot of the rocks and set off again for a sprint, in one direction then the other, to recover my equipment left on the headland. A first aid kit is among all my junk. The animal chattered during my short absence, but did not move a hair, or a feather in this case.

— You're perfect, a model patient. I'm going to treat you now. Just hold the stick, okay? Please don't scratch me.

I'm gently spreading his injured wing, unfolding it to get to the point of blood flow. It has an impressive wingspan, at least two meters. That's incredibly large for a male specimen. I disinfect his wound by looking into his eyes to see his reaction. He's always docile, his intense gaze directed at me. I notice then that his eyes are not entirely bright yellow as usual, they also have a hint of chocolate that makes them strangely... human. Decidedly, this bird of prey is full of surprises. Faced with his stoicism, I try everything for everything.

— Big boy, be quiet so that I remove the ball. I'll be quick, I promise. I'll sing you a song I learned when I was little. I'm sure you'll love it. It went something like this:

The raptors come through here

The raptors come back this way

They turn and circle in the air...

Like real war planes

The raptors come through here

The raptors come back this way

They turn and circle in the air...

Like real war planes!

I grab a pair of tweezers and plunge them into the

sweaty hole while singing. It won't take long, the bullet being visible since I cleaned the wound, but I have no doubt that it's painful. However, the eagle remains motionless even though its talons have tightened around its wooden prey and its hallux, the equivalent of our thumb, has sunk deep into the stick, the only sign of discomfort. Fortunately, I quickly grasped the foreign body with the pliers and pulled it out with a sharp movement. After such a painful ordeal, stopping the bleeding with cornstarch, which was all I had on hand, was child's play. Once this first aid is complete, I catch my breath. I hadn't even noticed that I was holding my breath until that moment. The cooperation of this animal may have been exceptional, but I was still stressed. Eagles are wild animals and their reactions can be unpredictable.

Chapter 7

Apenimon

It was my first gunshot wound, and I hope it's my last. Cayla, I like the sound of her first name in my ears, was very attentive, and the song she was humming made me smile in my heart of hearts, but the operation to remove the bullet was no picnic and required all my concentration to prevent a false movement of my eagle. My animal would never hurt her on purpose, but the pain makes him nervous and contracts his muscles unconsciously. My pretty vet regularly looked into my eyes and it was as if we were connected. It was a very intense moment and she did a really good job. It won't be long before my wound will be completely healed thanks to her care and the magic of Ottawa. I will then be able to take human form again and hug her in my arms to thank her. Although, I'm not sure she'll agree. She might be a little shaken to see an eagle metamorphosing into a naked man. Although that last point may work in my favor. I'll have to think of a new plan to approach her, as the chance encounter in the forest seems to be compromised.

— Come on, big guy, one more manipulation and I'll leave you alone.

Ah, looks like she wasn't done with me yet. Several times she passes a strip over the top of my wing and then wraps it around my chest to immobilize my broken bone. It's useless since my humerus started to heal as soon as she took the bullet out, but she doesn't know that.

— There's my pretty one. In a few weeks, you'll be good as new. You'll be able to get back on the road and fly as good as you did before. You're really lucky that vet Cayla's around here!

A veterinarian. That explains her dexterity. My companion is perfect, I couldn't have asked for a better one. She's beautiful, sweet and she loves animals to do such a job. She will easily find her place in the Ottawa tribe and her specific medical skills could be very useful. We heal quickly, but in case of injuries like mine, with foreign bodies, we are forced to go see a veterinarian off the island who doesn't know our secret, and he starts asking questions. I think he's tired of treating supposedly wild animals in the midst of his clients' dogs and cats. Having a veterinarian on the island, knowing the whole story, will be a blessing.

— It's not a branch, I suppose you'd prefer a high pedestal to rest on, but I promise you can sleep safely in my trailer. I'm looking out for you. Nobody's going to hurt you anymore.

Cayla strokes my head with her fingertips, and

I feel my eyes close on their own. It's been a trying morning and I'm finally with the woman I've been waiting for years. I can give myself a little rest. I have the impression that this is the beginning of our life as a couple, I will never fall asleep without her again.

I wake up much later to the changes around me. Fatigue took me by surprise and my sleep lasted longer than I expected, plunging me into an almost comatose state that obscured all the noises around me. First, the sun is fading in the sky, then a tent is set up right next to my makeshift transportation and finally, Cayla is out of sight, but I can hear a slow breathing coming from the igloo. She too must have been exhausted from her day and sleeping under the stars next to an eagle must not be part of her fantasies. Maybe that will change in a while, who knows. But she took care of me in my sleep. I'm covered with a little blanket. She was afraid I was cold, a great raptor that could pierce my prey with a single claw. Looks like my eagle caught her eye. He looks good, has an extraordinary build and behaved very well with her during her care.

I turn my head abruptly towards the grove when I hear whispers. Two different voices. Thanks to my keen eyesight, I can make out the two men from the restaurant grill, gun on their shoulders, who speak so softly that I can't understand the words they're saying. I was not mistaken about the culprits and it looks like they are coming to get their prey back. It was probably easy to find me, the trailer having left deep gullies in the undergrowth. A simple treasure hunts. I'm tempted to cut them to pieces, but I don't want to put Cayla in danger. If she sees their faces, she'll probably want them convicted. As a vet, and working for the MFFP, she'll never want to let poachers get away with murder. The best thing is, those two idiots are rushing to take me in without waking her up. They had to wait a while for her to fall asleep in order to go unnoticed.

That's it, they've finally made up their mind. They throw the blanket over my head and wrap me in it before they start running, with me as a load on the back of one of them. Luckily my wound is closed, because these two are so lacking in delicacy.

— The woman didn't see us and she has already treated the bird. You see we did well to wait.

— Yeah. You were right, it was a good plan and it saved us time. You're still lucky the bird of prey's alive. I told you to wait for it to land before you shot it. It fell from a height.

— I was impatient and it was fun to watch it struggle like a fish out of water to stop its fall. He bounced up and down the trees pretty good. Anyway, if he was tired, all you had to do was catch another one.

I'll have to think about getting them to pass up the urge to shoot animals before I give them bad company. The main thing is that my soul mate hasn't woken up. I know enough about her to be able to find her and a plan is already starting to sprout in my brain. I'm not going to go to her, she's going to come to me. On my territory, it will be all the easier to seduce her, and all I will have to do is convince her never to leave again.

The pair of idiots have managed to break into this protected zone with their pick-up truck. They took advantage of a wide space between the trees to park there. Decidedly, nothing stops them. My porter puts me unceremoniously in a cage in the back, as I had planned, and the vehicle sets off as soon as they have covered the cage with a tarpaulin. Perfect, under cover of the tarp, I am free to do what I want. Including metamorphosing. Hmm, it feels good to get my legs and arms back, even if the space is cramped. The gas that served as a bandage hangs at my feet, not having resisted the change in size. I cover myself with Cayla's blanket, smelling her jasmine perfume. I could escape immediately in the form of the eagle, but if they notice, they are able to shoot me again, and once was enough for me.

When the vehicle finally stops, I turn back into a raptor again just in case, but the two companions don't even take a look at their captive before leaving I don't know where. I open the cage by sliding the metal rod that keeps it closed. I sneak out of my pen and put my head under the tarp. It is now pitch dark and we are in front of some kind of shelter on the shores of Lake Kipawa. It seems to be a regular stop for them. I can see them through a window, ready to sit down and eat without worrying about their captive. On the walls, heads of endangered animals hang like macabre trophies. In the next room, I guess cages of all sizes, capable of holding all kinds of animals of different sizes. Unquestionably, they are not amateurs, just idiots. They are the typical example of the little hands that allow animal traffic to flourish in the region. They have no conscience and take pleasure in martyring defenseless animals. This place is despicable. I have seen enough and I do not have time to waste with the vermin of the human race. So much for my vengeance, I'll just denounce them, it will always be this way to win for the planet. I'm taking flight without further ado, Cayla's cover stuck in my talons.

Chapter 8

Apenimon

Before getting back to my car, I made a quick detour through Cayla's camp to make sure she was okay. When I got there, she was still sound asleep. I was thinking of giving her back the fluffy stuff still stuck between my claws, but I couldn't bring myself to part with it. This is a priceless memory of our meeting and it will keep me waiting until she comes to me. So I took the direction of my car, keeping it between my paws. With my cell phone in hand, I called the authorities directly to tell them the location of the poachers' refuge. There is no question of letting these barbarians continue their crimes with impunity. They are quite capable of killing another eagle when they notice my disappearance.

After the nap I took near Cayla, I'm in great shape and make the trip back to Manitoulin Island in one go, heartbroken at the thought of walking away from my bride, but also full of joy at the thought of seeing her again soon.

Home at last. It's good to be back in my environment and my mountain. I was gone for a short time, but I missed it. I love this island, its peaceful life and my comfortable home with the tribe. And at least here nobody's shooting at me. I was tempted to go to tyee right away and get him to help me put my plan into action, and then I realized no matter how open-minded my leader is, waking him up at 5:00 in the morning would probably be a bad idea before I ask him for a favor.

So, I'm still gnawing at the brakes until 7 a.m., when our chief goes out for a daily lynx ride, just before the tourists wake up. I metamorphose to reach him faster and I struggle with my eagle for the first time in my life, as he finds that my plan is not going fast enough. He wishes to join our soul mate without delay, even if it means returning to Lake Kipawa to do so. He is already in need of his touch; Cayla's caresses have literally electrified him. I understand him, I share his feelings. I can still feel the delicate touch of her phalanges on my plumage, like a drug I know I can no longer do without.

I find Tyee with Achak, as often, in their animal form, in the park next to the tribal chief's house. Their lynxes look very much alike, all in grey fur with black spots and glacier blue eyes. The only difference between them is that Achak is slightly smaller than his brother, which does not make him a less fierce fighter. His last fight with Takhi to defend his girlfriend is proof of this. He was fast and merciless, worthy of a warrior. We turn into men in a shower of sparks.

— Back so soon, my friend? You were quicker than I thought, a true Don Juan. Where is your companion? Have you ever left her alone? You told us you'd introduce her to us as soon as you got back.

— Yes and no. I did find her, and she's far too far away from me, Tyee. That's why I'm here today.

Achak interrupts us without giving me time to explain what I expect as a favor from the tribal leader.

— I had a vision of you wounded, being healed by a woman. I assumed she was your soul mate and that you would take her home.

— You could have warned me I'd get shot!!! It hurt like hell.

Achak widens his eyes in surprise and looks contrite.

— You got shot? I didn't know how it happened. The spirits were vague about the nature of your injuries. I focused on the fact that you were with someone and that was the main thing. You know that every event in life happens for a reason, don't you? What did you bring that bullet with you?

— My wife.

Ah, the spirits. They're clever and a little treacherous, but nothing happens by chance.

— Of course, it doesn't. If I'd known I'd get shot,

I'd have avoided this area to avoid the poachers and missed the point.

The shaman nods his head and Tyee takes over.

— So, your better half rescued you?

— She took exceptional care of my eagle. She's a veterinarian and a fervent animal lover.

They both smile with all their teeth. They both know what it means to meet her feminine ideal.

— A soul mate of great value Apenimon. You are very lucky.

— Yes, I'm well aware of that. She works for the MFFP.

— The Ministry of Forests, Wildlife and Parks?

— Yes. And that's where you come in. I know you've long refused their request to move to the island. I'd like you to call them and bring her here.

— They've been wanting to set up a rescue center in the cup and saucer area for years. I've always put the project on hold for fear they'd find out that all the animals around here aren't as wild as they seem. We already have enough of the vet's suspicions on the mainland. A thorough observation by connoisseurs of animal behavior would inevitably reveal anomalies. We take the shape of our totems, but we don't have the behavior, only the abilities and certain instincts. It is a symbiosis of man and beast, both physical and mental.

— I understand your position, but it's not a problem if my girlfriend is running the centre, as she will soon be aware of everything. She's going to be part of the tribe and she's going to know the magic of ottawa.

My chief and his brother are taking some time to think about it.

— I don't see why not. Achak, any objections? You're going to turn down another stranger's arrival on the island? Your gut tells you she may be a threat to you?

Tyee is teasing. He likes to make fun of his brother's mistrust when the last "bad" stranger to land on the island turned out to be his girlfriend.

— I won't make that mistake again. I won't make that mistake again. I won't trust blindly. But the question does not arise in this case. She is no stranger since... what is the name of your soul mate Apenimon?

— Cayla.

— Since Cayla will be joining the tribe very soon.

The chief consents.

— AGREED. I agree. I'll call the MFFP to arrange for your wife to come. They'll be thrilled that I'm finally acceding to their request. And surprised. I'm going to need a good reason for this turnaround. What's her last name?

That's where things get complicated. I hope they

won't give up on the gaps in my information.

— I don't know, I'm sorry. I'll remind you I was in an eagle when I met her. I couldn't discuss it with her. I only know what she told me while she was treating me.

— A monologue to calm your beast? She's smart, very smart.

Indeed, my future companion is quick-witted and resourceful.

—Shouldn't be too difficult to identify her, though. Her name is Cayla, she's a veterinarian, recently hired at the MFFP and, I think, French. She had a bit of the same accent as Isabelle, although some of the intonations were slightly different.

— Okay. (chuckles) That should do it. There can't be too many people who fit that description. I'll contact them later to arrange for her to come over.

— Now, please.

I'm insistent, but being away from my wife is both mental and physical torture. However, I have to respect my boss and therefore qualify my words.

— Now that I have found my companion, it is difficult for me to be separated from her. Patience is not my greatest quality and my raptor has been giving me a hard time since we returned home.

— I understand your Apenimon problem, but understand mine. Where do you think I would have put my cell phone?

Achak laughed.

— I do have a suggestion...

— Shut up, brother. I don't want to hear anything that comes out of your mouth.

Actually, we're all three naked. I'm laughing heartily with my friends. It feels good and I feel more relaxed since I realized Cayla was coming to my house soon. Once she's on the island, I'll never let her leave again.

<u>Chapter 9</u>

Cayla

Like the day before, my alarm clock is early, but instead of taking the time to emerge, I rush outside my tent to see my feathered camping companion. This bird has stirred something inside me. I don't know how to explain it, but I felt an inexplicable connection with him. Moreover, these unusual reactions piqued my curiosity. He touched me so much that when he fell asleep, trusting me, I covered him with the blanket that my grandmother made for me so that he wouldn't be cold. That's a load of crap. A bird of prey that's cold outside? You're really a beast, my poor girl, it's still his natural habitat!

The MFFP trailer is still next to my tent, but it's empty. No bird of prey, no blanket, nothing. It's like I dreamt yesterday's events and nothing happened. That's impossible, I didn't go crazy during my short stay alone. Like Robinson Crusoe, I made up an imaginary friend... Nonsense. I'm completely delusional right now! The eagle does exist and he had a broken wing, he couldn't fly away. Even getting off the trailer would have been complicated; I would have heard it for sure. But what am I saying? He couldn't walk away, he's a bird!!! I still look around, behind the groves and the young hemlocks, but no trace of greenhouses in the ground. On the other hand, I do see traces of hiking boots on the edge of the trailer and going back to the opposite side of my camp. Considering the size, huge feet, these are not my footprints. The only possible conclusion is painfully obvious to me. The poachers have found it. What a fool! I shouldn't have left him alone. They only had to follow the wheel tracks left by the trailer to get back to my camp. A simple treasure hunt. I was careless and they found him. They took him right out from under my nose without me even noticing. I feel like crying. This beautiful eagle will end up in a cage or worse, stuffed, with his head hanging on the wall of a despicable collector. I'm going to throw up. I lean forward, shaken heartily. It's not the first time I've lost a patient, I'm a vet, not God, but it's the first time I don't accept it, that I find life unfair. I hiccup, but it's a waste of time, my tears run down my cheeks and crash to the ground, like my heart. Why does it hurt so much? I feel like my chest is being torn apart. Even Richard's betrayal didn't hurt me that much.

There's no point in staying here. I'm having a hard time coping and I've decided to leave. Might as well leave this cursed place. I may not be able to help yesterday's eagle anymore, but maybe I can save the others from the killers roaming this forest by alerting the relevant authorities and informing the MFFP. After all, that was the purpose of this mission: to identify and address gaps in eagle protection. However, I had not envisaged that the problem would be the killing of these poor animals. I was thinking more of a tourist influx that would make them flee or soil pollution from wild dumps. I shake my head in frustration at my own naivety, throw all my stuff in the trailer and turn back to the 4x4 I left at the edge of the forest at the beginning of my expedition. I can't help but be on the lookout for the slightest movement or cry that sounds a bit like an eagle's cry, just in case a second miracle happens and I stumble upon it by chance. After all, this eagle is lucky, considering its fall yesterday. Unfortunately, there's no sign of him. Arriving at my vehicle several hours later, I have to face the fact that I will probably never see him again and the dull pain in my chest increases by one notch to that certainty.

My first phone call is to the authorities who tell me that they have already been warned at dawn this morning and have called all the protagonists. They still want me to send them my testimony as soon as possible in order to complete the case against them, as the poachers are going to appear in court. Others other than me were present at the scene even though I did not meet any hikers. Maybe my eagle managed to get away and these other hikers found him and came to his aid. I have to hold on to this idea to hold on to the shock, incongruous as it may seem.

My second call is to Clara, my project manager.

— Cayla! How are things at Lake Kipawa?

— Pretty bad. I saw some eagles, but poachers shot one of them.

— Oh, my God! Oh, my God! Oh, my God! Are you okay? Are you okay? Just stay away from them. Don't go up against them. Some small groups are very violent when caught in the act.

— Don't worry, I won't. I didn't even see them. I treated the eagle, but it vanished into thin air.

I can't stop my voice from shaking.

— You sound shaky, Cayla. Get back to headquarters. Anyway, until we're sure the mission is safe for personnel, it's cancelled. Stop by when you get to the facility, we'll debrief.

— I'll do that. I'll see you then.

It's time to get out of here. This forest I admired so much when I first arrived seems sinister all of a sudden, and as sad as I am. For my first solo mission in this new job, it's a total fiasco.

— Hello, Clara. I'm here.

— I can see that. Feeling any better? You sounded all worked up on the phone.

— Yeah, I'm fine. I'm fine.

— That's good, because you've been in a lot of demand today, I can tell.

— That busy? From who?

— Well, first of all, your old boss at the zoo.

Richard ? What the hell does he want from me? I keep a neutral face despite the anger bubbling up inside me. Even from thousands of miles away, he continues to harass me.

— What did he want?

— I don't know. I have no idea. He asked to speak to you and didn't leave a message when I told him you weren't here.

Then everything is for the best. I have no desire to hear what he has to say to me, any more than I want my new boss to know about my love affairs.

— Who else has asked after me?

— that's where I'm waiting for an explanation from you. Tyee Pontiac.

She's looking at me and obviously waiting for me to say something, except I don't know what. I frown, think, but no, I have absolutely no idea who this gentleman is.

— Am I supposed to know him?

— That's what I assumed. He's in charge of all the parks on Manitoulin Island. I've been harassing him for years to agree to have a rescue centre set up on his territory, and he's always refused. In fact, no, he did not say no outright, but he would postpone the project until a later date without giving me a good reason. So, imagine my surprise when he called me this morning to tell me that he agreed to let this project go ahead on the condition that a French veterinarian named Cayla would take care of it.

I am still forbidden. What is this story again? I'm sure I don't know this man and I had never set foot in Canada before joining the MFFP. I don't even know where the Manitoulin Island that Clara tells me about is.

— Excuse me ? Why me?

— When I asked him that question, he said that the spirits demanded it be you and that if I really wanted to do this, I had no choice. Either I send you, or the center ends up dead.

I must be making a strange face because Clara has a smirk on her face as she stares at me.

— Spirits? You've got to be kidding me.

— I thought it was a joke, too, but if you don't know Mr. Pontiac, then all I have to do is believe that explanation. This is an island inhabited primarily by native Americans, so pack your bags and study your legends.

— I'm going alone again? I must admit that I am not a fan of camping and I am not reassured to relive the same experience as in Temiscaming.

— Yes, you're going alone for the moment, a team will join you if the project comes to fruition. But Tyee assured me that he would provide you with a guide on site. And no backcountry camping this time, either. You'll be staying with one of the locals. Go home and sleep in a real bed. They're expecting you early tomorrow afternoon.

At least they know how to organize themselves on this island. This mission has a better hospice than the last one, although I'm puzzled by the fact that my presence is being requested by spirits.

— All right, then. I'll talk to you soon. I'll fax you my report on Lake Kipawa within the week and keep you informed of my progress in Manitoulin.

Chapter 10

Apenimon

My soul mate is due to arrive on the island today and I'm excited. I miss her very much. It's becoming a physical pain. I really need to see her, but Tyee wouldn't let me take her in. He made his point as a tribal chief and a park warden, and I had nothing to say no to those arguments. He also vetoed my request that she live with me. My chief thinks it would be too hard for me to be in her presence twenty-four hours without being able to touch her, to claim her. He may not be wrong, but I don't want her to stay with another male. Anyway, being separated from her is a pain so a little more or a little less... but Tyee didn't give in. Still, Cayla's mine! We finally found a compromise: Cayla will go to Achak and Isabelle's until my companion decides to come and live with me. Soon, I'm sure. She felt the connection with my eagle, I could see the trouble in her eyes. She will feel the same way about me. And I will be her guide. I've been uncompromising on this point. How can I seduce her if I don't spend a minimum amount of time with her? And there was no way she was going to spend her days alone with someone else. Besides, I know the territory like the back of my hand, both from the sky and from the ground. I'm going to show her my mountain and the eagles that nest there through my eyes. I'm sure she'll fall in love with the landscape. She has to, it's indispensable. I won't be content to sleep with her blanket on for several nights. It has kept me waiting until today, her jasmine scent still floating on it, but it won't be enough for me for long. I have experienced her hands on my feathers, now I want to feel her hands on my skin and her lips on mine.

I can't wait any longer. I'm going crazy knowing she's on the island and I can't get near her. I don't care about Tyee, I'm going there and I'll take the consequences if my leader doesn't appreciate my disobedience. I join the Pontiac brothers at the shaman's house and see Isabelle and Cayla who are already having a great conversation, a priori about their personal experience as expatriates. All heads turn to me when I arrive and Achak snickers I don't know what remark to Tyee's attention. He must have guessed that I wouldn't be waiting quietly at home. After all, he wasn't very patient when he met Isabelle either. He spent all his time spying on her as a bobcat. For the sake of discretion, he'll be back. He doesn't really have a lesson to teach me. Anyway, I don't care. My gaze never leaves my companion for a second. Tyee ends my trance by speaking.

— Cayla, this is Apenimon, your guide. Apenimon, this is Cayla, the person sent by the MFFP.

I look into her eyes and find her even more beautiful than yesterday. She has put on a comfortable outfit for the hundreds of kilometers in the car and the simple black t-shirt and jeans suit suits her well. I shake her hand and a warm current flow up my arm. I'm sure she feels it too, her arm gets goosebumps.

— It's nice to meet you, Cayla. I look forward to showing you our island and its treasures. You'll see, this land is full of mysteries just waiting to be discovered.

It's hard for me to pretend I don't know her, as if she didn't represent a special person in my eyes and in my heart. The only thing I want at this moment is to hold her in my arms.

— Nice to meet her too. I can't wait to get to work. These gentlemen, as well as Isabelle, explained to me that we were on Amerindian territory. I don't know what that means to me, I must admit. And the fact that spirits have demanded my arrival is quite disturbing.

— The most important thing to know is that animals are sacred in Manitoulin, they have a lot of importance in our culture, just like the spirits.

That gives him a huge smile. She is dazzling, with luscious lips of a beautiful natural pink that I long to kiss as soon as possible.

— Why am I here if wildlife does not need protection?

She has a sharp mind and a critical eye. Perfect.

— Species always need more. Don't you agree with me?

— Of course, I agree. I would do everything I could to help you and make their living conditions even better. But if no one minds, I'll begin my mission tomorrow. The journey has exhausted me.

So, Isabelle is taking matters into her own hands. This woman has blossomed since she's been with us, and even more so since her pregnancy.

— Come with me. I'll show you to your room and you can freshen up.

— Thank you very much. Thank you very much. One last thing before I leave you gentlemen. I prefer to be introduced to you on a first-name basis. Otherwise, I feel like I'm at least 50 and I don't feel that old.

I love his repartee. I'm detailing it again from head to toe.

— You're certainly not.

Once those ladies get home, the Pontiacs don't waste a second taking my side. Tyee starts the fight.

— I told you to stay home. Doesn't your name mean anything anymore ?

— Apenimon means trustworthy and I am, no

doubt, but this is my soul mate, not a tribe affair.

Then Achak adds a layer to it, this false token.

— You didn't even have the patience to wait for someone to call you.

— Don't lecture me, old brother. You forget that I fly around the island several times a day on guard duty and that my bird of prey has the sharpest eyesight. Remember what you were like after meeting your wife. I watched you prowl around Tyee's for days, mostly when Isabelle was out with the little one. I assumed it was because I didn't trust her. Your lack of openness to strangers is legendary. It wasn't until later that I learned the real reason. You watched your bride like a psychopath. Someone else in her place would have probably gotten scared.

The older brother laughs his head off while the shaman pouting. He still has the decency to be contrite.

— Decidedly, it's impossible to have a private life or secrets on this island.

— I'd say it's more of a tribal problem. Everybody's interested in everybody else's life, it's a hobby in itself. I guess everyone in Ottawa already knows we're welcoming a newcomer and the real reason why she's here?

— All the clans are happy for you. We all know how lonely it's been for you these past few months.

<u>Chapter 11</u>

Cayla

I watch the three men through my bedroom window. Okay, let's be honest. I'm peeping at one in particular. Boy, he gets me hot in all the right places. And when he shook my hand, I thought I was melting in place. He's all muscle but not swollen on steroids. On the contrary, he's tall, much taller than me, who's not small for a woman, and yet he's a good twenty centimeters taller than me, and his biceps stretch the fabric of his shirt in a very appetizing way. I admire his matt skin, his three-day beard and his deep eyes that seem to notice the smallest details in a second. I could see his eyes slowly caressing my body from top to bottom, lighting a fire in his path.

— Is everything all right? You look pensive.

I'm startled, caught in the act of spying. I drooled so much in front of Apenimo that I forgot Isabelle was in the room.

— I was just dozing off.

She, in turn, approached the window and took a look outside. My cheeks turned red under the sparkling gaze of my compatriot who was not fooled for a single second. Her voice of a contained laugh confirms it to me.

— Yes, that's probably it, fatigue.

Even if I've been caught red-handed, I might as well take advantage of the opportunity to find out.

— Apenimo has someone in his life?

Isabelle smiles at me with all her teeth.

— No, he's single. But not for long, I think.

I shrug my shoulders. What took me to be so direct? I'm no prude, let alone a goody-goody, but I don't throw myself at the first good-looking guy that comes along, either. I don't really know how I feel, let alone what I want, right now. There's something really wrong with me since yesterday.

— Well, we'll see. I just went through a breakup. Maybe I should give myself some time alone.

Isabelle's standing next to me.

— Can I ask you what happened? Don't feel obligated to answer me, especially not now. Sometimes I'm too curious.

I wave my hand to let her know there's nothing wrong. I brought it up, and Isabelle seems to be the perfect confidante.

— My ex, who was also my boss, cheated on me after a year of relationships.

Her face darkens for a moment, giving me a glimpse of her own experience that doesn't seem any more appealing than mine, before it lights up again at the sight of Achak below, chatting with his brother and Apenimon.

— Ah. If it makes you feel any better, the Ottawas of this tribe are unique and very different from the men you may have known. When he gives himself to someone, it's all out, no pretense, no compromise.

I don't really understand where she's going with this and

I'm not sure I want to. I'd rather change the subject.

— How pregnant are you?

— Five months. And this little guy's already a real wild one, just like his daddy. A real ottawa.

I envy his bumpy belly and the secret he's got inside. I hope to know the joy of having a child one day. If I can find the right man, the man who'll want to take the plunge with me... Suddenly I am melancholy, remembering all the hopes I had placed in Richard, and seeing raptors in the sky doesn't help. They remind me of my eagle, and the dull pain in my chest gets worse. Isabelle must have sensed my change of state of mind as she discreetly withdrew.

— I'll let you get some rest before we go to the table. Call me if you need anything.

I lie down on the bed with the soft mattress and as I close my eyes, I see a beautiful yellow look with the reflections of hot chocolate filled with intelligence. My eagle never ceases to haunt my mind, whether I am awake or not, and my heart bleeds for him and his sad end. When I returned to the MFFP, I took the time to contact all the animal centers and veterinarians around Lake Kipawa, but no one had heard of a wounded eagle. I guess his luck had changed. My last hopes that it was hikers who had found it collapsed when I hung up my phone.

Achak and Isabelle are a very close-knit and warm couple. The tribe's shaman, as some people call him, looks at his wife with a gaze mixing tenderness and deference. I would not be surprised if he stood up to kiss the ground she walks on. I can only dream of such a sincere and deep love. To dream of it, and to hope for it more beautiful. And what about all the attentions he has for her, or the protective gestures on her belly which contains, I quote, her greatest happiness.

It is time to return to a less sensitive subject for my already tormented little heart. After all, I am not here to play games, but to work. The question crosses my lips before I am fully aware of it.

— Are there a lot of eagles in this part of Canada?

Achak looks at me with interest and a lot of curiosity.

— Why this question?

— They are my favourite animals.

— Are they?

— Yes, I even have a collar shaped like an eagle.

Then I show them my pendant hidden in my top, a gift from my parents for when I come of age.

— That's interesting. Yes, there are a few that nest on mountain tops. Apenimo can take you there. It's right next to his house. His windows overlook the trees they live in, he likes to look at them.

I'm more and more attracted to that man. He's handsome as a god and loves eagles.

— Then he and I should get along well.

Achak thinks that I don't know what in his eyes that tells me that he knows things I don't know and that he won't tell me anything about the secrets he knows..

— I'm sure he won't. I think you two have a lot in common. Starting with an unconditional love of nature and birds of prey... Well, this promises to be interesting.

He's totally promoting his friend and Isabelle nods in agreement. It's cute, but it's useless, I'm already almost conquered even if I try to keep a cool head. This man has the physique of a sex god and, as far as I know, an altruistic spirit. After all, I'm free as a bird and there's nothing wrong with doing good to yourself. This mission may take a long time, setting up a wildlife rescue centre from scratch takes time. I have to study the fauna as a whole and make an inventory of all the species present on the island in order to adapt the premises and equipment, and then hire competent people to run the structure. It will take me weeks or even months if the building has to be constructed. But perhaps they already have some rough drafts of the answers to these problems?

— Achak, what are your needs in terms of the centre?

— We regularly find injured animals and are forced to take them to a vet off the island, which takes time and the health of the injured can worsen during the journey. There are no animal care professionals on Manitoulin and that's a real constraint.

— Why are there so many injured people? The Ottawas are very respectful of wildlife, it seems to me.

— You've done your homework, Cayla.

— I had to. The spirits have requested my presence! It made me curious about your culture. But information is scarce. You're a very secretive community.

My guests look at each other, communicating silently, just with their eyes, and when they agree, the shaman takes over.

— To sum up, the ottawa worship Mother Nature and pray to animal totems, which are the equivalent of your gods.

— You do more than just love life. It is the very basis of your existence.

— Yes, it is. It's a part of us. And to answer your initial question, tourists are not necessarily as careful as we are and regularly cause accidents involving our animal friends.

— All right, then. I'll do my best to improve things on the island then. I'll be proud to contribute to the preservation of your way of life.

<u>Chapter 12</u>

Apenimon

I'm picking up Cayla in the early hours of the morning, like we agreed the day before.

— Hello, Cayla. Sleep well?

— Great. Where are we going this morning?

— I'll give you a choice. Do you want to start by observing the different species of mammals or birds?

— Let's start with mammals. My boss told me that the center should be set up along the Cup and Saucer trail. I'd like to see the site.

I'm surprised at her choice, I thought she'd be eager to see eagles, but don't argue with that. By the way, it's only the first day of the visit.

— Of course, let's go.

It's only half an hour's ride, but it gives me a chance to strike up a conversation.

— What country are you from? You have a very nice accent. A bit like Isabelle.

— You have a good ear. You guessed it. I'm French, like her, but I come from a region much further east, close to the German and Luxembourg borders.

— There's a lot of natural space there?

— Not really, no. It's a rural department, but nothing like Manitoulin.

When I arrive at my destination, I choose to start the hike in the opposite direction, in order to reach the promontory overlooking waterfalls and a belvedere more quickly.

— What kind of animals can you come across here?

— The fauna is very varied on the island. There are moose, deer, beavers and black bears, but also lynx, wolves, foxes and eagles.

— And they all live in harmony?

— Yes, they do. Each to his own territory.

She observes the flora with interest, the thousand-year-old cedars and the steep cliffs, raving about this grandiose landscape, while I only have eyes for her.

As the week progresses, I show her the island and the picturesque places on it: Bridal Veil Falls with its crystal-clear waterfall, Kagawong Lake, the second largest lake on the island and teeming with salmon, and the Bebamikawe Memorial Trail, where she literally fell in love with guide dogs. I was even jealous of all the attention she gave them. She kept petting them and saying sweet words to them. I wish I had been in their shoes!

But it's time for me to take my wife home and since she's not making up her mind, I'm going to provoke events by going to pick her up today.

— I noticed your necklace. It represents an eagle, if I've seen it correctly.

— Yes, it does. It was a gift from my parents, because they know they're my favorite animals.

She responded by subconsciously caressing the pendant. I

think it's a recurring gesture for her. I watched her do it regularly all week, whenever a raptor flew by.

— You might want to see some in this case. I know the perfect spot.

— Achak tells me that your house overlooks eagle territory. I'm actually curious to see it.

— I'm curious to see it. Then we'll head for the mountains.

It feels strange to drive up there. Usually I'm there in a few wingbeats. But being in the presence of my soul mate is far from being unpleasant and it gives me a chance to get to know her better.

— How did you come to work for the MFFP? You haven't told me yet. You're a long way from home.

— It all started with a zoo.

It must be a good memory because she looks happy and her beautiful eyes sparkle.

— You intrigue me. Tell me all about it.

— Actually, there's a very large zoo near my parents' house: the Amneville Zoo. The first time I went there, I couldn't have been more than six or seven years old. I was literally charmed by all its animals, from ferocious tigers to small lemurs, I thought I had entered a magical world with magical beings. And when I saw the spectacle of the raptors... I can't even put into words what I felt that day. I couldn't take my eyes off the birds for one second from the beginning to the end of the show. I didn't want to go home anymore. I had decided that I was going to pitch a tent in an alley at the zoo and that from then on, I would live here. That's when my father told me the sentence that changed my life. He said, "Choose a profession related to animals, work hard, and one day, your dream will come true. And that's exactly what I did, and I did it, and I did it. I didn't live in the zoo, but I practically did. I was hired as soon as I finished school and I spent days, and sometimes nights, with my feathered and furry patients. But life evolves and the following events made me reconsider my desires and future prospects. And here I am in Canada.

She didn't dwell on the "events," but I sensed annoyance in her voice. I don't have time to dwell on the fact that we have arrived. My curiosity will have to wait.

— Your house looks great. I've noticed that almost all the houses on the island are made of wood.

— The vast majority, yes. Remember, we're close to nature. So, we use natural materials and objects in our daily lives.

— And why choose to be isolated like this? You're out of touch with the rest of the tribe.

— For them.

I take her hand and lead her to the front of the house, where my garden ends with the abrupt fall of the promontory. The open view shows, down below, hundred-year-old fir trees with eagle nests on top.

— Eagles. They are so majestic. I can see why Achak said we have something in common. If I have to settle down somewhere one day, this is exactly the kind of landscape I will choose to see from my windows. You're as passionate as I am. I had noticed it the previous days when I heard you talk about the island so passionately, but this place is the ultimate proof.

Oh, perfect. She won't be hard to convince when I ask her to move here. I'm on the right track. All I have to do is start explaining my uniqueness.

— It's more than a passion. The eagle is my totem animal and I'm just like him. He represents courage, truth and honesty. My name is Apenimon, "he who is trustworthy", and I am the warrior of the tribe, charged with defending it. I am a policeman for the same reason. The eagle is, in fact, my alter ego. I have a very strong bond with him. I don't know if you understand what I mean. Have you ever felt a similar bond with anyone?

I can see right away that she understands, but I didn't expect the sequel. A tear rolls gently down her cheek.

— Yes, it does. I met a raptor at Lake Kipawa on my last mission. You should have seen him. He was very special. One of a kind. But I lost him. He was wounded. He'd been shot. I treated him, but he was gone when I woke up. He probably died because of poachers.

Does she mean me? What are the odds that she nursed another eagle in Kipawa besides me? Close to zero. Which means she thinks I'm mortally wounded and cries. Idiot. I should have let her know I was all right. I should have waited for her to wake up before I flew away. She imagined the worst and her sadness is palpable.

— Hey. Don't be sad. Eagles are very hardy. He probably made it.

I hug her and wipe away her tears with my thumb. Despite the circumstances, feeling her velvety skin under my fingers is a real aphrodisiac. She raises her head and, without my preparation, places her lips on mine. Her kiss is soft, sensual, intoxicating, and I cross the barrier of her teeth as soon as she allows me to. Her tongue caresses mine and her hands grasp my neck as I press her hips against my manhood. If I listened to myself, I would undress her to discover her voluptuous body, but I don't want to rush through the process and I have some revelations to make before taking her to my bed. She takes her tongue out of my mouth and kisses me tenderly a few more times before taking a step away. It was too short and at the same time, so intense. I would have liked this moment to last a little longer, but Cayla decided otherwise.

<u>Chapter 13</u>

Cayla

Wow. That was kissing. I'm so glad I jumped in. Apenimon's amazing. When I met his gaze, I was captivated by his molten chocolate eyes with golden highlights and I let my desire run free. The comfort he brought me is welcome after my confession about my eagle. His slight caress of the back of his hand on my cheekbone allows me to get back on my feet. Well, almost.

— Are you feeling better, my sweet?

There is so much emotion in those few words, a mixture of tenderness and worry, that my throat tightens again, but an eye on his face relaxes me instantly.

— Thank you. Thank you. Thank you. I needed comfort.

— Whenever you want, sweetheart. I'm ready to be of service to you day and night.

I shake my head and giggle, but the offer is tempting, and his smirk on the face tells me it wouldn't be much of a chore for him.

— I'll think about it. But right now, I have to work. Can you give me a moment? I'm afraid I'm a little distracted by your presence. You're very confusing.

He's wincing. Damn, I misspoke and I'm in a hurry to make up for my blunder.

— In a good way. But I have to work. I'm going to watch the raptors and take notes.

He loosens up and turns his heels.

— I won't be far. Shout if you need me.

I watch him walk away, and if I listened to myself again, I'd put my hand on his ass. I wasn't joking, Apenimo literally puts my senses into turmoil. The more time I spend in his presence, the stronger the temptation. It's a mixture of desire, I'm obliged to squeeze my thighs in his presence, but also of respect. I like the way she thinks, the way she lives.

He joins me a few hours later. My work has progressed well, I have scribbled a multitude of pages with the behavior of eagles, my indications and ideas of additional protections that could be put in place. Only I forget everything when the handsome Native American eagle stands on my back and hugs me, resting his head on my shoulder, to look at the landscape with me. I could get a taste for it very quickly.

— You look like you've been working hard. You've been taking notes for hours.

— Yeah, it's been a busy day. I'm swarming with ideas. This place inspires me.

Apenimon drops a kiss right under my ear. It's intoxicating, intoxicating, and frightening. It's taking on so much importance in my life, so quickly. I can't imagine coming home without him. It is for this last reason that I decide to end this interlude reluctantly.

— I should go home. I don't want to keep Isabelle and Achak waiting for dinner.

— Or you could stay here and eat with me.

The idea is tempting, very tempting, but I'm not sure I can be reasonable with him and I want to take the time to work through my feelings. I've only known him for a short time despite the incredible attraction I feel. Everything I feel is mixed up. So, I turn into his arms and put a kiss on his mouth before walking to the car.

— Tomorrow night, if you want.

— I won't forget. Tomorrow night, you're mine.

There's so much possessiveness in his voice. So much promise, it gives me the shivers.

— About dinner.

— For a start.

I like her perseverance. And I'm looking forward to it, too. He jogs up beside me and opens the door, kissing me on the corner of my mouth as I pass. It seems it's just as hard for him as it is for me not to touch each other. In fact, he holds my hand all the way home in a comfortable silence.

I suddenly come down from my cloud to the vision that is offered to me upon our arrival. I feel like I'm taking a bucket of ice water in my face. Richard is on the porch of my hosts' house, detonating in this universe so natural, so simple, with his grey suit well cut. I tighten up, pinch my lips, my discomfort is so obvious that Apenimon doesn't fail to notice it and, following my gaze, tightens up in turn.

— An acquaintance?

— You could say that.

I don't wish to expand on the subject. I don't know where I'm going with him, but I very much want to find out, and Richard won't come and spoil it. I wish my ottawa would have stayed in the car and turned back just as dry, avoiding an unpleasant confrontation, but I'm not that lucky. He goes around the car to help me get out and keeps my hand in his, interlacing our fingers. His gesture escapes no one, but after all, I have nothing to hide.

Isabelle makes the introductions in front of my eloquent silence, after a glance leaning on our joined hands.

— Richard, this is Apenimon. Apenimon, Richard, the former boss of Cayla.

I thank Isabelle in thought to have skipped over

the rest, but at the moment when the two men shake hands, my ex doesn't hesitate to spread my private life, adding to it, of course.

— I'm also her fiancé, actually.

I'm choking on my crooked saliva and don't have time to catch up with Apenimon when he abruptly lets go of my hand and immediately drives off again. The last thing I see is the pain in his eyes so expressive. Isabelle's right, ottawa is unique. When he gives himself over, it's all of it. Apenimon's expecting more than sex, a lot more, and my ex just made a hell of a mess. I got my voice back and now I'm pissed off.

— What the fuck are you doing here?

— I'd like to talk to you, honey.

— There is no more honey, dickhead. You cheated on me. It's over. It's over. I thought I made that pretty clear before I left.

— Looks like you wasted no time replacing me.

No, but is he fucking with me right now? Is he blaming me?

— And you didn't even wait until you were separated to do it!

I didn't even notice Isabelle slipping away, but it's better this way because I feel like things are going to get worse with that dickhead, and the tone might get louder. What right has he to come here and declare that he's my fiancé in front of my friends and... Apenimon, whatever happens to me?

Richard must have become suicidal since I left, because wanting to take me on when I'm so pissed off seems like a good idea to him. I push him away without a moment's hesitation and realize that I'm angry, yes, but because he drove Apenimon away, not for his betrayal. I no longer have any feelings of love for him. My heart has a crush on a certain Native American now, and Richard's untimely presence has made my mind clearer than ever before in a flash. I almost have to thank him.

— We were good together, Cayla. We could pick up where we left off.

Yeah, well, no thanks given in the face of so much hypocrisy.

— You mean with me looking at your intern on your dick?

He doesn't even seem sorry, just embarrassed to be caught.

—No, of course he doesn't. I'm sorry, darling, I made an unfortunate mistake and you should never have seen it. Midlife crisis makes men do stupid things; you know that.

No, I don't know, and I think it's a pathetic excuse. It's like I got my bad mood on account of my period!

— Not all men behave the way you do, Richard. There are some lovely ones in this world.

— Because you think this Api... I don't know what, will be different?

He didn't dare disrespect someone he barely met for a second, anyway! My Native American gave me more attention and tenderness in one week than he did in six months. In retrospect, I think our relationship had been going downhill for a while, but I refused to see him. I had been dreaming of a fulfilling life as a couple, but it turned out to be just that, a dream. I raise my hand to Richard to shut him up.

I'll stop you right there. Apenimon is an incredible man who means a great deal to me and there's nothing here that doesn't concern you. You should leave without wasting any time.

— Are you forgetting our plan to have a child? I'm willing to do it for you.

He thinks he's doing me a favor? He thinks he's the only man capable of procreating with me? You're kidding, right?

— That's where you're wrong. This is what I want, and I don't want a man to make a baby for me, I want a man to make a baby with me. Now get out of here.

Chapter 14

Apenimon

What a cold shower! Cayla's engaged. She's already found the man of her life and it's not me. I found my soul mate and I'm already losing her. The spirits have played me well! The spirits... Achak told me I should prove myself. But I haven't proved anything yet. Only Cayla has opened herself up to me as the strong, brave and sensitive woman that she is. All I did was get shot looking for her, which she doesn't know, show her the island, and be charming to make her want to stay. In the end, I made the same mistake as Isabelle and Achak. I ran away. I didn't let Cayla explain herself and I didn't try to understand the situation. I turned away from her and set sail at the first obstacle. That's hardly worthy of the persevering fighter that I am. And like Achak, I'm taking the risk of losing the person most important to me. She is irreplaceable in my heart and I must do everything to conquer her, even if I have to put my pride aside and accept that, for the moment, Cayla does not belong to me, which is a very unpleasant idea.

I turn back without further prevarication and return to the one to whom I belong without reservation, even if the reciprocal is false. I find her on the terrace where I left her, with her fiancé, this idea scars my heart, in the middle of a lively conversation. Her eyes, so affectionate when she looks at me, seem to throw lightning bolts in front of him. She takes my hand as soon as I get close to her, warming my soul with this simple gesture.

— Apenimon, I am not engaged. Richard should never have come. I do not wish his presence.

Obviously, the other intruder could not remain silent during this defining moment between me and my savior.

— I'm still here. Perhaps you could wait before you jump on the first one.

She's facing such a sudden movement that I'm forced to hold her back to stabilize her. She now seems overwhelmed.

— Have you always been this dumb? How could I not see it? Now get out of here.

I like its volcanic nature. Exactly what I wanted to get from my wife.

— Cayla, we're not done talking...

I get in the way when this intruder tries to grab Cayla's arm to bring her closer to him.

— Do not touch her.

He then starts acting like a rooster and deliberately

provokes me.

— I did more than just touch her arm, buddy. I've been...

He doesn't have time to finish his sentence that my fist goes straight into his jaw, making him close his mouth with a snap of his teeth. He could file a complaint against me and as a representative of the order on the island, I am likely to be suspended from my duties, but at this point I don't care. Achak chooses this moment to go out and take this idiot out of his territory, and hopefully out of the country, manu militari. With his lynx's hearing, I'm sure he followed the exchange from the beginning, ready to intervene if necessary. He probably figured that the time had come if he didn't want blood to stain the wood at his entrance. It's unbearable to imagine hands other than mine on the perfect curves of my beautiful. It was one too many remarks for my self-control.

Cayla seems even more irritated, if that's possible.

— I'm sorry. I'm sorry. I'm sorry. I shouldn't have hit him, but I can't stand the disrespect. I'm sorry. I'm sorry.

— What are you apologizing for?

— You're angry with me. You're angry, I can see that. I didn't have to get involved.

She strokes my cheek and her fingers squeak on my beard.

— It's Richard I'm mad at. You're... perfect. Thank

you for coming back. I couldn't bear it when we part on a misunderstanding.

I'm sure now she feels the same way I do.

— I'll always be there for you. But I must confess I'm curious to know what you found for her... And why was he here since obviously your story is over?

She drags me to a bench on the porch and sticks to me, her chest pressed against my arm. I hug her waist and run my hand through her silky hair, dipping my nose into her jasmine scented locks. That smell has become my drug. I took every opportunity to sniff it during our excursions, every time I helped her up a cliff or down a slope, I bent over a little more to smell it.

— Richard's the zoo manager I was telling you about. I hesitated at first because I didn't want to become the cliché: the employee sleeping with her boss, but I finally gave in to his advances. We stayed together for several months and I must admit that at one point I hoped that our relationship would evolve and that we would one day start a family.

I reach out and imagine her carrying someone else's child. The only baby she will have in her belly will be an eagle. I will accept nothing less.

— I realized he'd never think of me as anything more than an easy lay when I caught him cheating on me. I left the country a few weeks later to start a new life. And then I met you.

She puts her head on my shoulder and I could be like that for days.

— Do I scare you?

She seems worried while she waits for my answer.

— No, she doesn't seem worried. Why should she be?

— I feel... so many things. It's so sudden and strong.

— You're forgetting I'm an ottawa man. I believe in magic. And I believe in us. I care about you more than anyone else ever could.

I kiss her feverishly, I want to devour her, to discover every part of her body with my fingers and my mouth. Except that we're still at Achak's house and he reminds us by clearing his throat a few meters away from us.

— Sorry to interrupt you lovers. I just wanted to let you know that I drove your old boss to a motel. I strongly suggested he take the first plane out to France tomorrow morning.

My sweet seems relieved.

— Thank you, Achak. I couldn't have stood her presence much longer.

— You're welcome. You've become a friend and no one bothers my friends. Especially not an arrogant, self-righteous man. Now both of you get off my terrace. You'll end up shocking my wife by eating your face like that.

We're laughing and I'm not afraid to take my partner home with me.

Chapter 15

Cayla

Now that the misunderstanding has cleared up and I have taken stock of my feelings, I wish to spend as much time as possible with Apenimon. I'm not the kind of person who respects the three-date rule before spending the night with a man. Without being an easy girl, I know what I want and I enjoy every moment. And by cheating a little, we have the three meetings: we've been together for seven days even if they weren't official dates.

He brings me into his home for the first time and I discover a clean but warm place. The large beige leather sofa is turned towards the huge bay windows overlooking the garden and the tip of the fir trees below, with the eagles hovering in a circle above them. The open kitchen is very convivial, all in light wood, and my ottawa is heading there with the probable intention of preparing me food. It's lovely, but I'm not hungry for food, I'm hungry for him. I've made my decision and I'm taking the consequences. I care about him more than I should. So, I surprise him by approaching behind his back, putting my hands under his shirt to explore the smooth, firm abs he covers. His muscles contract under my palms and his nipples rise as my hands pass by. He then turns around, grabbing his top in the process to pass it over his head. Looks like we're on the same wavelength. His flat belly attracts me and I follow the thin line of hair from his belly button to his jeans. Apenimon moans and straightens me up to capture my lips in a devastating kiss.

— You drive me crazy, my beautiful one.

He follows the line of my jaw with the tip of his tongue and pecks my neck, creating a path of goose bumps in his path. My top joins his on the ground and I'm glad I wore a black lace bra this morning, although my underwear doesn't seem to interest him at all. He's trapping my nipple with the tips of my teeth, titillating it with his tongue, and I can't stop my head from tilting backwards.

— I need to talk to you about something important, sweetie.

I don't really feel like talking right now. I've got something else on my mind.

— Um, later. Show me your room.

I wrap my leg around his hip and he grabs my butt so I can wrap the second one around his waist. Thus hooked, I kiss him and taste his tongue as I feel him move. His private space is in his image, raw and warm. A polished wooden chest of drawers and a matching bed, the light coming in through the bay window opening on the same side as the living room. It is superb. But what catches my eye is not the outside view, but what sits in the middle of the huge bed.

My blood freezes in my veins and my heart stops beating while Apenimon does not notice my trouble and touches my back. I would know that blanket a thousand times over. My grandmother made it for me when I turned 18. It's one of a kind. And the last time I saw it, it was covering my eagle at Lake Kipawa. I put my feet back on the ground, my legs in cotton wool. I feel like I'm outside my own body. I can't believe the only possible explanation and I have to clear my voice to be able to speak.

— You were at Lake Kipawa.

He looks me in the eyes, confused. He probably thought I'd never find out. He played me for a fool with his love of eagles. He loves them so much, he shoots them to sell them. No wonder there's a lot of wounded animals around. He has to practice on those poor animals.

— Yes, he does. But, uh...

— You took the blanket.

That sounds like an accusation, because it is. He lays his eyes on the bed, then comes back to my face, and his shameful expression confirms my suspicions.

I'll explain it all to you. It's not what you think...

I cut him off and walk away from him, unable to look at him now that I know who he really is. He lied to me about everything. He's a traitor among his people.

— You don't really like raptors. You're a poacher. You're the one who took my eagle.

I couldn't stop my tears from coming out. I turn to the window and see the eagles soaring, making me double my sobs. My bird of prey will never know such happiness again. He must be dead or in a cage by now. I've got to get out of here before I collapse. Apenimon tries to hold me when I grab the blanket, but I duck his grip and flee through the opening of the chamber, finding myself in the garden. I have been here before, but I can no longer think and I don't know which direction to take to reach the security of Achak's house.

— Cayla, wait. This isn't what you think it is.

— What did you do to her? He's, uh...

I can't even pronounce those words that hurt my heart. I keep retreating while Apenimo continues to advance, pushing me to the edge of the precipice.

— The eagle is fine. The eagle is all right. I promise you. Come to me, Cayla, it's dangerous here.

Indeed, one false move when Apenimo tries to grab my hand causes me to slide over a rock and I fall over. My cries and those of my Amerindian mingle, forming an echo during my dizzying fall.

— CAYLA.

— APENIMON.

I believe my end was near when a high-pitched cry rang out just above me, making me open my eyes that I hadn't even felt close, and allowing me to see an eagle diving in my direction and grasping the blanket tightly against me. The claws pierce the cloth that holds on despite everything, and I note with relief and dismay that the bird slows my fall somehow thanks to the blanket that I am holding on to with all my might. The bird of prey is obviously struggling to support my weight, but it is holding on, and even if I fall to the ground a little hard, I don't crash to the ground in a bloody heap as I should have done. The bruises I get after a steep descent of more than forty meters are a lesser evil.

The eagle awkwardly lands next to me, visibly exhausted by the superhuman effort it has just put in, and I then notice something incredible that soothes my heart and leads to a host of unanswered questions. Those eyes, pure yellow with chocolate flakes. I couldn't forget them, I even dreamt about them at night. It's my eagle, the one I nursed in the Old Forest, and it's in great shape. That's impossible, I must be mistaken, he has no wounds left. His wing is strengthened and he has all his feathers. And yet, with such expressive eyes and such an intangible bond between us... I'm sure it's him.

— You're alive and completely healed. And you saved me from certain death.

I approach him without fear. I'm convinced he'll never hurt me. I'm convinced of that. He is unique and out of the ordinary. What eagle flies to your rescue to prevent you from crashing to the ground? My fingers glide over his fine feathers and it's as if he's shivering.

— You are so beautiful.

The way he looks at me seems so smart, so human. And how is it that he's so close to Apenimon's without being in a cage? Did he manage to escape? Did Apenimon set him free? Or was I mistaken? Apenimo gave me the benefit of the doubt about Richard, and it's up to me to do the same and learn the full story, hoping I won't be disappointed.

Chapter 16

Apenimon

I love his hands on my feathers as much as I love his hands on my skin. I was having a wonderful time before she saw the blanket on my bed. I knew I had to talk to her before things went any further between us, but I couldn't resist her hands and lips on my body. Nevertheless, I must reveal myself to her now if I don't want to lose her forever. She took me for a poacher, which is already an insult in itself even if I understand her suspicions, but above all, she ran away from me, the spark of desire in her pupils extinguished, replaced by contempt and horror. I move away from her a little so as not to hurt her and take on a human appearance in the middle of a rainbow sheaf, under her dumbfounded gaze.

— But how??

Her mouth is open like a fish out of water. It's quite comical.

— Can I give you a hug? You scared me so much. I need to touch you; hold you close to me to make sure you're okay. Please? Please? Please? Please? Please? Please? Please?

She nods her head, seemingly unable to speak, and touches my face in disbelief, as if to make sure she's not dreaming. Once I've huddled by my side, my back leaning against a tree and the damaged blanket with my claws hiding my anatomy, I'm ready to fully reveal myself to the woman of my life.

— Do you know that I'm a native american, an ottawa, and that my totem animal is the eagle?

I'm waiting for her approval and move on.

— Our tribe is very powerful and possesses ancestral magic: I can take the form of the eagle at will and I also have a tenfold healing capacity.

— You turn into a raptor?

I'm giving his brain time to consider this new fact. I must admit that it's hard to grasp, even when you've seen it with your own eyes.

— You didn't remove the eagle. You're the lake eagle.

A statement, not a question.

— The cover gave me away, didn't it? I couldn't part with it.

— The cover set me off, it's true, but what convinced me in that crazy theory were your eyes.

She's looking into mine.

— Gold flake chocolate, the exact opposite of the eagle I rescued. Unique and captivating eyes.

— You saved my life that day at the lake. I couldn't have healed if you hadn't taken the bullet out of me. It's the one thing magic can't do anything about.

— You let me do it. Your eagle never mistrusted me.

— You trusted him, too. You trusted me.

— I feel... it's difficult to explain.

— A connection ?

— Yes, a connection. A strong bond between the eagle and me. I feel like I'm close to him. As close as I feel to you.

She frowns.

— Why did you keep the blanket on? It has no value other than sentimental. And what were you doing by the lake? You went far away from Manitoulin. You told me you didn't like being away from Manitoulin.

I smile at his curiosity. These are indeed important questions for the future.

 The blanket is yours and you're important to me. What are you willing to believe?

She smiles at me and strokes my arm around her waist.

— I just saw an eagle metamorphosing into a man. I'm willing to accept a lot coming from you.

— I was at Lake Kipawa looking for my soul mate, and I found you.

I touch his collar, without which I could not have achieved my goal.

— I spotted you through your pendant. It sparkled with the reflections of the sun and drew my eagle to you.

She took it in her hand and moved it under the warm star that was waning on the horizon.

— All shape-shifters have one person made for them. The one for whom our hearts beat and who is the center of our universe. That's why you feel this bond between us. We're meant to be together.

— Achak and Isabelle!

— Yes, but how do you know that?

— The way they look at each other and understand each

other without even talking. Unconditional love, without half measures.

— They're soul mates, yes. Achak has marked him, there will never be anyone else for him.

— Marked?

— He bit him to signify to everyone that they've given themselves to each other. An indelible mark and an eternal bond. There's no divorce here.

— Are you going to bite me too?

— We're not from the same clan. The Pontiacs are bobcats, I'm an eagle. My clan doesn't bite its partner. Our mark is signified by a claw.

She grimaces, but she doesn't withdraw. On the contrary, she sits astride me and I can't hide the erection that's been aching since we embraced under the tree.

— The eagle's claws are sharp. It must be painful.

It rubs against my crotch and my head is at the level of its still half-naked breasts, intoxicating my senses. I have trouble concentrating.

— No, it's an aphrodisiac.

I put my hands on her hips to try to immobilize her, just to get to the end of this conversation.

— You're really turning me on right now.

— Mm-hmm. Maybe I'm doing it on purpose. You're being all hard on me.

She's licking my skin on my collarbone and coming up under my ear, always rubbing my manhood through the fabric. No use resisting, the time for small talk is over, and anyway, I have no secrets from her anymore. I undo her bra and suck her breast into my mouth all while kneading the other one. They're warm and soft, but there's still too much thickness between us. She says the same thing to herself because she lifts just enough to remove the blanket. You little rascal! I want to have better access too. I take advantage of her movement to lift her up a little more and take off her pants and panties. She is already all wet for me, ready to welcome me. I was going to take my time, but she decides otherwise and literally impales herself on me. The pleasure flows through my veins like a tsunami. I try to control myself to make this moment last, but she completes my control with a simple command.

— Mark me.

I make slow back and forth movements, to begin with, but the pressure rises quickly and her moans of pleasure excites me even more. I find it very difficult not to obey her on the spot, only it's not a trivial act, it's a lifelong commitment and I want to make sure she's aware of that.

— Are you sure about this? Are you ready to be my wife for all eternity?

— Without any hesitation. I fell in love with your eagle the moment he trusted me, and with you the day Tyee introduced us.

She moves frantically on top of me and I pound her now without mercy. The moment I feel the first signs of orgasm tingling in my lower back as Cayla's vagina contracts over my appendix, I scratch her leg, making her my companion. This made her come instantly and I, in turn, go into ecstasy.

Once we come down from our post-orgasmic euphoria, we realize that we are naked, outside, and visible from the top of the cliff. Caught up in the passion, the place didn't matter to us. I wouldn't change this moment to the level of a real eagle, but we could have been more discreet.

— Please tell me the eagles above our heads are real animals, not members of your family.

I burst out laughing and reassure her.

— They're wild birds of prey. But it's better to get dressed if you don't want to be caught.

— Except that you don't have any clothes on.

Indeed, I came in the form of an eagle. She puts her bra and panties back on after one last wet kiss on my mouth, then looks at her leg. Three deep scratches bar her calf. I can't see her face and can't figure out what she thinks about it. I hold my breath and my eagle looks at her carefully.

— Do you mind having a scar?

The radiant face she turns towards me reassures me immediately.

— I find it very sexy. It's a part of you and your eagle. I'm all yours.

I touch my mark with pride and my eagle cackles with pleasure in my head. I wrap my sweetheart's shoulders in the blanket after she puts her pants back on. It's a sacrilege to hide such a gorgeous body, but I don't intend to let her dress for long, just long enough to get her back into bed and resume our frolic, this time making it last.

— I'm going to run home in a hurry to get dressed and I'll pick you up in the car.

— All right. All right. All right. All right. All right. Make it quick. I want to see your room again.

I'm more than up for it. I'm making a complete makeover without wasting a second, but my eagle doesn't take off right away. He takes the time to strut his stuff in front of our girl and even begs her to give him a pat on the head, which she does.

Chapter 17

Richard

This Native American threw me in the first shabby hotel he came across, as if I were a simple tourist. No, but no kidding. He wrinkled my suit, too. I put on my Armani to show off to Cayla, and she preferred to watch the hillbilly in the corner with his jeans and T-shirt. If she thinks I'm going to let it go, she's dreaming. Ever since she left, the zoo staff has been giving me a hard time, and it's time for it to stop. No one respects me anymore and that stuck-up intern who told everyone about Cayla's remark about the size of my genitals! Since then, I hear them whispering behind my back and I've caught them several times talking about micro penises. It's humiliating and it's gone on too long. Cayla has to go home with me to prove to everyone that I'm a good catch, that she was wrong to dump me, and most of all, she has to tell them that I'm a good catch. She ruined my reputation. I've never been caught before and I got careless, overconfident. She wasn't the first young girl I've jumped into my office, but it's the first time my bedtime has had such repercussions. Since that incident, trainees are no longer willing to do anything to get hired, they spend their time giggling and some have even gone to the HR department to complain. They say I'm too clingy and I look at them too closely. I'll give you a damn! I don't want to stare at them, I want to fuck them.

But I have to be discreet. I may be the director, but I'm

not untouchable. I'm accountable to the shareholders, and I better nip it in the bud before the next board meeting, or I risk losing my job. And for that, I need some face-to-face stability, and Cayla is perfect for the role with her marriage and baby wishes. I want to get laid, not start a family, which is why I had a vasectomy years ago. When hallway noises started coming out months ago about me liking women who were a little too young, dating Cayla proved to be a great way to shut them up. I plan to use her again this time. Especially since if I'm at this point, it's partly her fault.

For starters, I've got to get that Apenimo out of the picture. I've seen the way those two look at each other, and there's no way that guy's going to get in my way. No one's going to stop me from going back to France with Cayla. And I'm sure the two guys squinting in the lobby can help me do that. They seem to care about him, too. I heard them ask the receptionist where he could find him, and she wouldn't answer. If I help them, the feeling can be mutual.

— Gentlemen, I think I can help you.

— I don't see how you can help?

— I believe we have a mutual acquaintance. Apenimon?

— Apenimon Wima. We need to speak to him. Do you know where we can find him?

With their military-style uniforms and zero balls, these guys are scary. A good-looking killer, and the vehicle I see outside with cages and a gun safe won't contradict me.

— I can probably find out. What exactly do you want with him? Just to talk? Because I'd be happy if he disappeared for a while.

They look at me up and down, squinting, suspicious.

— I just have a score to settle with him too.

— It's negotiable. Get us his address.

— Don't move from here.

I leave the hotel lobby and go to the grocery store across the street. This island is tiny. Everybody knows everybody, I guess.

— Hello, beautiful lady. Sorry to bother you, but my friend Cayla asked me to meet her at Apenimon Wima and unfortunately, she forgot to give me the address. She gets a little dizzy sometimes.

— Cayla, Apenimon's companion?

— Yes, his companion.

That word is scratching my mouth. She'll never be his companion. She's going to come back to France with me and get it over with.

— Of course, I'll make a plan for you. He lives in the mountains. His house isn't hard to find, it's right on the top.

There it is. Easy as pie. Too bad I don't have more time, this chick is just what I like, small, with tits and ass. I don't care about the face; I just want to have something to hold on my hips to pound her like a bitch. I reluctantly leave towards the two companions who are waiting in front of their car and hand them the paper where the indications are written down.

— That's it. And if he's with a woman, don't hurt her, she's my girl.

— This guy stole your girl? Is that why you're helping us?

I'm nodding my head.

— Some people are toxic around here. The natives are vicious. He's not the only bad guy around here.

— Don't worry, she'll crawl back to you when we're done with the other one.

All right, fine. Now all I have to do is wait quietly for her to come back to me. Maybe I'll take this opportunity to go back to the mini-mart, here. I've got a good mind to test a Native American girl to see if she's as slutty as the women in this country. Besides, it'll help me relax and have a good time.

<u>Chapter 18</u>

Cayla

— It's nice to see you too, handsome. But I can't sit around with my breasts out in the open all day and it won't be long before nightfall.

My eagle takes flight with a last cry in my direction. He's gorgeous and, as I suspected, quite unique. I can't believe what just happened. I witnessed an incredible phenomenon, pure magic, I literally jumped on Apenimon, and I got married, well, the Ottawa equivalent, which is definitive. And I have no regrets. I regret nothing. I've never been happier in my entire life. I take one last look at the cliff top and then head off in the direction that my... husband pointed me in. It's going to take me some time to adjust. I quickly fall onto the small path he told me about and wait for him to come with the car, and my shirt if I'm lucky enough for him to think about it. It shouldn't take long. As the crow flies, getting home is child's play.

Only, unlike my bird, I'm not a lucky person, and male voices come to me from the corner of the path. Awesome, great outfit to meet my in-laws or tribe members. Very passe-partout and not at all flashy. And I was hoping to make a good impression so I could fit in easily. After all, I'm going to settle on the island and Apenimon is very respected here, I don't want to tarnish his image by getting caught in flagrante delicto of exhibitionism. I stop flogging myself when two hunters appear before my eyes. We are on a protected territory; the whole island is. And now I understand why. Animals are not necessarily what they seem to be here. A lynx may turn out to be a tribal chief and an eagle, my lover. I must intervene to prevent an accident.

— Good morning, sir. Good morning. I'm sorry to disturb you, but there's no hunting on Manitoulin Island.

The two protagonists are staring at me.

— I recognize you! Always getting in the way. We didn't come for you, but we're going to kill two birds with one stone. The guy at the hotel was right. There are pests here.

I don't understand what those two are talking about. How do they know me?

— You must be mistaken. We've never met before. I haven't been here long.

— No, you haven't. I'm not an idiot. You're the eagle thief. We were coming to kill the bastard that got us arrested. We should have guessed you were in on it.

Then I realize the identity of the two men facing me.

— Kipawa poachers!

— That's right, sir. And you're going to lead us to the one called Apenimon Miwa. I'm sure you know him. He gave us up to the cop and we'll make him regret it. No way he'll testify to get us thrown in jail.

Apenimon. Of course. He's the one who notified the authorities before I did. He was in a position to know what happened and to give all the details. There's the missing piece to the Kipawa puzzle. I must protect him at all costs as he would protect me.

— I'm sorry, I don't know anyone by that name. I don't know who you're talking about.

— Don't take us for fools. You want us to believe it's a coincidence you're on this path? There's only his house at the end of that road and you're half naked. He threw you out? Aren't you a good shot maybe? You should have stayed with the guy in the suit, he was ready to take you back and I can see why. Too bad we won't be able to honor the deal we made with him.

I shudder with disgust at the way they look at my chest and tighten the blanket around me. What does Richard have to do with this?

Apenimon

I just can't believe it. Cayla's finally mine. I marked her. She's my lifelong companion and has accepted the world of ottawa without batting an eyelid. I put on my clothes in a hurry, eager to join my soul mate and pick up where we left off. I want to spend the whole night in bed, with her huddled against me. The presentation to the tribe will wait until tomorrow. I've waited too long for this moment to agree to share her with the others right now. I'm about to get my car key when I'm interrupted by my phone ringing. I'll get past it, but I'm chief of police and this could be an emergency. I answer reluctantly.

— Hello.

— Mr. Apenimon Wima?

— This is he.

— I'm the officer in charge of the poaching case you reported at Lake Kipawa.

— How can I help you?

— I wanted to warn you in person that the poachers were released on bail early this morning. They know some very influential people and have even been granted a right of review of the case.

— Oh, I see. I see. So, they had access to my testimony and contact information.

— I'm sorry. I'm sorry. I could not oppose it.

— I understand that. Money makes a lot of things possible. Thank you for your call. I must leave you now.

Cayla

They approach me menacingly, pointing their guns at my head, when suddenly the man closest to me receives an eagle in the face. My eagle has come to my rescue and shows no mercy. He puts his claws on the hunter's face and drives his hallux into the eyes of the assailant, gouging out his eyeballs with a disgusting noise. Without wasting a second, I stand in front of the second man who tries to help his accomplice by pointing his rifle at my love. At this distance, my companion has no chance of survival. He told me, his weak point is the bullets. He cannot heal if a bullet remains in his body and if his heart or head is hit, I would be helpless. I have to save him again. I fight with all my strength, grabbing the gun with both hands to divert the barrel from its target. Unfortunately, the hunter is much stronger than me and pushes me against a tree, crushing my windpipe with the crossbow to put me out of action. Then powerful legs appear in front of my eyes filled with black spots due to the lack of oxygen and cut the tendons of my attacker at the wrists, putting an end to the attack. The men lie on the ground, moaning, trying to stem the bleeding from their wounds in vain. I would be inclined to pity them if I didn't know of their unhealthy intention towards the love of my life.

Tyee and Achak arrive in the meantime, followed by the mainland authorities who stop the hunters and perform first aid.

Achak rubs my back as a sign of support.

— Are you all right, Cayla?

I stutter, still shocked by the attack, and keep one hand on the head of the eagle who has placed himself at my side to reassure me.

— Yeah. Yeah, I'm fine. Apenimon intervened just in time. How did you know we were in trouble?

— A combination of circumstances. The authorities called Apenimon to warn him that the poachers had been released pending trial and had been given access to the witness' details by their lawyer. He called to warn me just before he came down.

— While the motel manager, our cousin, warned us that two men were asking questions, helped by your ex-boyfriend who was happy to harm Apenimon.

The Pontiacs interrupted their explanation as the police approached. They advance without taking their eyes off my eagle, who watches over me at my side. Indeed, it is a bodyguard who is out of the ordinary.

— Madam, you will have to file a complaint for assault and testify with Mr. Miwa for the poaching incidents at Lake Kipawa that were reported to us.

— I'll file a complaint, of course. But their primary intention was to kill Apenimon Miwa. They made that clear to me.

— Very well, it will be noted in our report. You'd better step away from that eagle. He can be dangerous. Both suspects are badly wounded. In fact, they'll be physically incapable of hunting again one day.

Well, that's good news. Two less psychopaths on the loose.

— You don't have to worry about me. This eagle is tame. He'd never hurt me. He's mine.

The police seem skeptical, but they don't insist.

— Oh, very well, sir. Then I think people would do well to think twice before attacking you.

They certainly will. That eagle has my heart just as much as I have his. We'll always protect each other.

<u>Epilogue</u>

Apenimon

Cayla's been living with me for a few weeks now, and it's wonderful. She's setting up the wildlife care center on the outskirts of the Cup and Saucer and it was agreed with the tribe that she will run it. Everybody welcomed her with open arms, normal, she still saved my life twice, and she seems happy. All that's missing from my dream is a child of hers. A little piece of her and me. I've known all along that she wants a baby, but I don't know if she's ready to go for it with me. Her life has changed so much in such a short time and she's been through so much.

Cayla

I've been waiting for Apenimo to make up his mind for days, but nothing comes. I am a woman of character and far from patient. I've taken the first step towards kissing, sex and branding, so why not keep it up. I find him on the couch, contemplating the eagles.

— Baby, can I ask you something?

I'm riding him, like I always do. I like to be close to him all the time. And this position reminds me of our first time and the brand that changed my life.

— I'm listening to you, sweetie.

He rubs my back up and down, lighting a fire between my thighs without even meaning to, and dips his nose into my cleavage.

— I know it's early, but after all, we're soul mates and you've marked me, so I don't see the point in waiting any longer. I'd like to have a child from you. A little eagle.

He immediately raises his head and his joy explodes in a wild, deep kiss.

— I didn't dare ask you. You make me the happiest man in the world. Techihila.

— I love you too, my beautiful eagle.

The end

<u>**Also By : Viginie T.**</u>

<u>Paranormal romance</u>

◊ Guardian Angels Series: - Connor

                               - Sean

                               - Nate

➔ The Ottawas Series :

- My Ottawa Lynx   - My Ottawa Eagle
- My Ottawa Beaver   - My Ottawa Bear

➔ Fallen Angels Series : - Dance my angel

➔ Colors of the Dragon

➔ Fangs to my blood

Facebook : Viginie T.

<u>Volume 3 : My Ottawa Beaver</u>

The Unexpected Soulmate

<u>Chapter 1</u>

Ahmik

It's been a tiring, not to say grueling, day. Since my parents decided to travel the world in search of God knows what, I had to take charge of the beaver clan and that's not at all what I wanted. I felt that at just 30 years of age, running my own wood home building business on this beautiful Manitoulin Island while enjoying the pleasures of life was more than enough for me. But the Great Manitou decided otherwise, and here I am in charge of the clan and the protection of the island's biodiversity, a role my family has held for generations. On this last point, however, I must say that the arrival of Cayla on the island, a veterinarian working for the MFFP, the Ministry of Forests, Wildlife and Parks, and incidentally the companion of my friend Apenimon, has greatly lightened my workload. I was able to focus my efforts on the rivers only, while she takes care of the plains and the mountains, even though I find she focuses a little too much on the eagles living there. On the other hand, the construction of the cup and saucer centre provides me with a comfortable income and work for several weeks. Especially with Cayla who has a clear idea of what she wants and is very demanding, to say the least. I wonder how Apenimon manages to support her! This woman leads him by the tip of her nose, or rather, by the tail, in my opinion. Great good to her, I willingly give her this pleasure that I don't understand. On the other hand, although my role as a wildlife warden has been considerably lightened, my taking over as head of the clan has increased my responsibilities towards the beavers. I am the one to whom they must turn in case of conflicts, difficulties or even a desire to talk. To discuss ! I am not an office man but a man of actions and this function weighs on me to the highest degree, only, it is my duty. The chief of the Ottawa tribe to which I belong, Tyee, only intervenes on the condition that I have not found a solution beforehand. He already has his own clan and business to manage, so he delegates as much as possible to the clan chiefs for minor conflicts, in other words, for the beavers, me.

The only advantage I found: the chicks fall into my arms in a snap. Not that I had trouble finding a woman willing to keep me warm the night before, but since I officially became the chief of the beaver clan, I have even more choices. I'm well aware that the chicks I pick up in clubs and bars are only interested in me for my money and social position, but since I'm only interested in their bodies, I don't care. All I expect from them is a good time and then goodbye and maybe see you next time, if the opportunity arises and the lady is not too clingy.